Lottery Lovers

Also in the *X Libris* series:

Lottery Lovers

Vanessa Davies

LIBRIS

An *X Libris* Book

First published by X Libris in 1998

A CIP catalogue record for this book
is available from the British Library.

ISBN 0 7515 2307 0

Photoset in North Wales by
Derek Doyle & Associates, Mold, Flintshire
Printed and bound in Great Britain by
Clays Ltd, St Ives plc

X Libris
A Division of
Little, Brown and Company (UK)
Brettenham House
Lancaster Place
London WC2E 7EN

Lottery Lovers

Chapter One

'*JUST A QUICK* drink, Sara. There's no harm in that, surely?'

Sara Kingsley hesitated at the door of her office. It would be nice to go to a wine bar and relax with her boss for half an hour before the long drive home. She would miss the rush hour and, more to the point, postpone the moment when she had to confront her husband, Guy. They'd parted on bad terms that morning and she was dreading seeing him again.

But one look at Jon Marsh's smiling, handsome face convinced her that it would not be a good idea. She knew he fancied her. More to the point, she fancied him back, and that was dangerous. When she'd taken on this job she knew she would have to be on her guard against her new boss's rampant libido and low, sexy voice. Once before she'd tried to mix business and pleasure. She'd managed to keep her job and marry the man, but you could only play that game once and get away with it.

As she left the building, Sara thought about Jon's plus points. Tall, lean and with just the kind of hazel eyes and dark blond hair that reminded her of her first boyfriend. Then she thought about Guy: equally tall, well built, with dark curly hair, sultry brown eyes and a seductive grin. She'd have found it hard to choose between the pair of them four years ago, before she'd married Guy. What a shame a girl couldn't have her beefcake and eat him too!

The drive south of the river was tediously slow and, for a while, Sara daydreamed about having an affair with her good-looking boss. He was in his mid-thirties, divorced and not looking for another permanent relationship. If she were in the market for a lover he would be the obvious choice, and although she had no intention of following through it did no harm to fantasise, surely?

What if she had said yes to that drink? They would have gone to their local wine bar, Vin Extraordinaire, where they could have mingled anonymously with the crowd then settled in one of the private cubicles. The place was made for discreet assignations.

Sara's mind drifted into the fantasy. Yes. They'd lean towards each other until their noses almost rubbed; their hands would touch as they raised their stemmed glasses of full-bodied wine while, below the table, their knees would brush intimately.

Jon would talk to her in that low, sexy tone that made her wilt inside. What would he say? There would be compliments, of course, the sort he handed out every day in the office: 'Like that new perfume . . . pretty lipstick colour you're wearing . . . looking very attractive in that blouse . . .' Other women despised such talk as sexist but, to give him his due, Jon had asked her at the beginning if she minded him commenting on her appearance. She'd told him she found the feedback helpful. After all, she did have to meet the public, and first impressions were important. As the months went by she came to value her boss's opinions on such matters. At home, Guy hardly ever seemed to notice how she looked these days.

But when they were alone, in that wine bar, she was sure that Jon's remarks would take on quite a different implication. He would be complimenting her not as his assistant, but as a woman. Sara felt her pulse quicken at the thought of those hazel eyes meeting hers with melting intensity. The wine would lower her guard, make her giggle more frequently and confess to things she would normally hide. Like how boring her sex life had become, and how long it had been since she had felt thoroughly satisfied in bed.

Would she really tell him that? A slow flush crept into Sara's cheeks as she sat impatiently at the wheel waiting for the lights to change from red to green. She imagined he might say something trite, like 'A woman as attractive as you deserves better, Sara.' At that point he might possibly take her fingers and press them to his lips, watching her all the while. She would giggle some more, look wary as a gazelle scenting danger, and he would assure her that he wasn't trying to persuade her to do anything she didn't want to do.

Not in so many words, perhaps. But his sultry tone of voice, his soul-searing gaze, the scent of his freshly applied aftershave combined with the subtle musk of his arousal would all be acting as hidden persuaders, nudging her ever nearer to the point of no return. After a few glasses she would mumble something about needing to get going and he would take her to the door, his hand at her elbow, then ask her if she was fit to drive.

As drunk with desire as she was with wine, Sara certainly wouldn't be in any state to drive. He would take control then, helping her into his car and driving with practised ease through unfamiliar streets. Sara had never been to his flat, although she knew he lived in Barnes. By the time she bleated her faint protest they would be almost on his doorstep.

'Thought you could do with some black coffee, to sober you up. Then I'll drive you home.'

'Oh, but . . .'

'It's no trouble. Anyway, we're nearly there.'

The flat would be small but tastefully furnished and immaculate, as if he'd been expecting her. The espresso coffee would be laced with brandy, neatly sabotaging its restorative properties. He would sit beside her on the extravagantly large settee with his arm spread along the back, perfectly in control while she was all jittery inside. She would make a fool of herself, blabbing and giggling like a schoolgirl while he responded with grave politeness to her idiotic ramblings.

She didn't know quite how the first move would be made. Perhaps, overcome by alcohol and the presence of a friendly ear, she would collapse in tears and need to be physically comforted. Or the conversation would turn to how attractive she was, how long he had wanted her, how she teased him on a daily basis just by being so unconsciously sexy.

Or he would merely sense the need in her and, confident of not being rebuffed, would draw her

4

into his arms and begin to kiss her, gently at first and then with increasing firmness until she could feel the passion growing in him, the urgency of his lust mirroring her own. He would start to caress her through her clothes, not making any move to undress her but making it more and more difficult for her to bear the barrier between his fingers and her flesh. She would start to unbutton her blouse herself, her fingers working with feverish haste, but he would gently enclose her fumbling hands with his own and then do the honours with slow care, slipping the garment gently off her shoulders.

Sara's breasts began to tingle at the thought of his caress, of his fingers homing in on the hard tips of her nipples through her lacy bra. With indecent haste she would clumsily attempt to unhitch the garment and again Jon would help her out, removing it gradually until her shapely firm breasts were open to his gaze.

'Gorgeous!' he would murmur, or some such epithet. Then his head would bend reverently towards them, filling her with wild trepidation as her libido was notched up into a burning hunger that would make her bold and shameless. She would want more of him then, her fingers probing into his shirt to find the hot smoothness of his skin with its downy mat of chest hair. Sara had seen holiday photos showing his tanned torso, so she knew just what to expect.

As the fantasy continued she could feel her fingers trembling on the steering wheel and knew she must be more careful. The traffic was speeding up now they were away from the river, and she had to concentrate more on her driving. Reluctantly she blotted out the erotic images from her imagination, replacing them with thoughts of Guy.

There was not much time to decide what to say to her husband when she got home. Things hadn't been going very well lately. With a shock, she realised that that was an understatement. The last eighteen months of their marriage had been decidedly lacklustre, especially in the sex department. No more bedroom romps on Saturday afternoons or Sunday mornings. No rushing straight into bed on Sunday evenings after Guy had been away on one of his weekend conferences.

Even when they did make love it was usually a rushed business, with Sara being more passive than she used to be, too tired – or was she too uninterested? – to play the sort of teasing games that used to drive Guy wild. What had gone wrong? She knew that it was more than just the usual settling into a comfortable routine that most married couples went through.

Money had a lot to do with it, of course. There never seemed to be enough, even with both of them working full time, and when Guy had bought himself a new suit out of the household account she had hit the roof. There wasn't enough left to pay that month's standing orders and she'd had to filter money in from her savings account, money that was supposed to pay for a week's holiday.

It wasn't much to ask, she thought gloomily; just a week in a caravan in Devon. The thought that they would be going there in June had kept her going through the bleak days of winter, but now she doubted whether they could afford it. It was too bad of Guy! He'd tried to make out that he needed a new suit for work but she had to make do with her old clothes, so why couldn't he? The thought of his selfishness pressed her lips into a thin line and made her hands tighten on the wheel.

But the following thought, that she and Jon might steal a dirty weekend together, brought a smile to her lips. Not that she could see him on a caravan site! Sara imagined a four-star hotel was the minimum he would tolerate. A luxury suite with a Jacuzzi was more his style. She sighed, picturing herself lying back in a tub of hot bubbles with a glass of ice-cold bubbles in her hand. Jon would massage her breasts with the foam, then slip in beside her to fondle her body more intimately . . .

A car swerved in front of her, crossing into the next lane, and Sara had to jam on the brakes. She cursed, her sybaritic mood instantly quashed. In five minutes she would be home and having to confront her erring husband. The prospect was not a pleasant one. Slipping into a side street, she decided to take a short cut and get the business over with as soon as possible.

Guy was awaiting her in a surprisingly contrite mood. He had cooked a curry, one of his specialities, and the smell greeted her along with his sheepish smile.

'Hullo, love. Look, I'm sorry about this morning.'

After averting her face from his kiss, Sara glared at him. 'So am I! What do you intend to do about the fact that we can't pay the bills?'

'I thought I'd cash in my premium bonds. Will that cover it?'

'But that's practically all your savings!'

'I know, but we have to pay the bills somehow, don't we?'

Sara took one look at his woebegone face and decided to give him a hug. He clung to her like a contrite child, and she felt resentment well up in her. His solution to their cash flow problem was strictly short-term. With so little to fall back on they had no way of coping if they fell behind again. She pushed him away and went off to the kitchen on the pretext of wanting a cup of tea.

The kitchen was shabby and in dire need of a refit, which only depressed her more. They had taken on a mortgage which they could only just afford in order to get a house, not a flat. Theirs was a nondescript 1930s' semi – not the kind of house she had ever dreamed of living in, but they had bought it during the housing boom and now the repayments were crippling them. She was slowly coming to detest the place.

'Fancy coming out to the pub tonight?' Guy asked hopefully, as he dished out the chicken korma he'd made.

Sara scowled. 'We can't afford it.'

'For God's sake, woman, we have to have *some* entertainment.'

'What's wrong with the telly? We've paid enough for the licence, and that stupid satellite dish you insisted on having. I don't know why you wanted it. You never watch the thing.'

'I do when there's a good match on.'

Sara could feel the tension building in her again. 'Well, I'm not coming out to the pub. If you want to squander your money on drink, that's up to you, but I have other priorities. Like putting food on the table.'

Sara knew that she was only making things worse, but she couldn't help herself. Something about Guy's expression irritated her greatly. He looked like a stubborn little boy who was determined to get his own way. It would be a relief to have him out of the house, so she wouldn't argue further.

He went out around nine, leaving Sara to do the washing-up. She put on the TV and began to watch an old film, set on the Californian coast at Malibu. Now that would be a place to visit with a lover! Days lounging on the warm beach, watching sexy young things roller-blading around. Nights living it up in Beverly Hills, where the beautiful people wined and dined in luxury beneath a star-spangled sky. The very idea of being in Los Angeles filled her veins with a kind of tropical heat and made her pussy throb with longing.

Absorbed in the film, she completely forgot that it was Wednesday, the night of the midweek lottery draw. They spent two pounds a week on the lottery, with Sara buying the ticket on Saturdays and Guy midweek. They always entered the same set of numbers, a selection of family birthdays.

The lottery programme had finished by the time she thought of it, so she decided to check their numbers on Teletext. As she flicked her way to the relevant page Sara's full lips were pursed in wry anticipation. What if Guy had forgotten to buy the ticket or, worse, decided not to buy one out of spite after their row that morning? And what if tonight was the night they would have won the jackpot? That would definitely be grounds for divorce!

The numbers at the top of the screen stopped

9

flipping and the lottery page came up in garish yellow, with the bonus ball in green. Sara stared at the spread of winning numbers. She scanned the whole line and her heart flipped. Holding her breath, she stared hard at the screen.

Surely they couldn't *all* be their numbers? But quite a few were, she was sure of that. Her mouth felt dry and she was clenching her fists as her heartbeat thundered in her ears. The numbers danced and swam before her eyes. There was her own birthday, fifteen, and Guy's, twenty-two. She went through the lot methodically, left to right. There was seven, his sister Penny's birthday, and eleven, his brother Mark's. Then there was Guy's mother's birthday and their own house number. The bonus was forty-six – they didn't have that. But they had every single one of the rest.

Sara wanted to scream, to weep, to run out of the house to the pub down the road, laughing and dancing all the way . . . but she did none of those things. Instead she sat mesmerised by the flickering screen with its stark numerical message, and read through the rest of the information like a zombie. 'Three winning ticket holders will share the midweek National Lottery jackpot of £4.5 million,' she was informed. The machine was called Lancelot and the set of balls was number seven. Lucky for some. Lucky for them . . .

Guy! It all depended on him now, on whether he had remembered to buy their ticket. What if he'd forgotten? The lump in Sara's throat reached painful proportions as she contemplated that horrible irony. Or what if, after putting down the same numbers for months on end, he'd decided to change them – just this one, fatal time?

She jumped up from the sofa and promptly sat down again. What should she do? The thought of confronting Guy in the pub was unpleasant, but she just had to know for sure. She could ring the Swan and ask him to come home straight away. Yes, that was the best option by far. The thought that he would presume something bad had happened made her smile. Let him stew for a few minutes; it would serve him right!

With trembling fingers she found the number for the White Swan in the phone book and dialled. Karen the landlady answered, eventually. For a few seconds Sara lost her nerve, tempted to replace the receiver without speaking. Then she was equally tempted to scream down the phone, 'We've won the lottery, we've won the lottery!' but she restrained herself just in time.

Rising panic made her voice waver as she finally said, 'Hullo Karen, it's Sara. Is Guy there?'

She knew how it would look, as if she were checking up on her husband. Well, let them think what they liked!

'Yes, darling. Did you want to speak to him?' The landlady's voice held more than a hint of curiosity.

'Er . . . no, it's all right. Would you just ask him to come home straight away?'

'Are you OK, love?' There was genuine concern in Karen's voice now. 'You've not had an accident or anything?'

'No, I'm fine. If you could just ask him to come home now, I'd be very grateful.'

The five minutes after she put the phone down were the most stressful of Sara's entire life. She knew that once she told Guy there was no going back. She tried to imagine how she would feel if he hadn't bought the ticket – then if he had. There was such a painful tension in her chest that she wondered if she were in danger of having a heart attack. Where was the joy, the elation that she'd expected to feel if ever they won the lottery? In its place was quite a different emotion: stark terror!

Sara couldn't understand it. Perhaps she would feel differently if she knew for sure that they had won. A share of £4.5 million: how much was that? A million and a bit each. She tried to work out how much income that would bring in if they invested it. A hundred thousand a year, and then some! They could blow the extra and just invest the million and they'd still be quids in.

The old-fashioned phrase brought her down to earth with a bump. It was something Guy's father used to say. He was dead now, but his mother was still very much alive and so were Mark and Penny. Suddenly that million didn't seem such a huge sum after all.

Guy's arrival interrupted her anxious reverie. The minute she heard his key in the door Sara rushed to greet him and fell into his arms on the verge of sobbing. It was no ploy. The tensions of the past few minutes had built up in her to such an extent that they had to have an outlet. For a while she babbled incoherently until Guy led her into the sitting room and made her sit down.

'What's happened?' he asked her, frowning. 'Has someone been taken ill, or what?'

She loved him for his simple concern. All the resentment she'd felt over the past few months melted away as she took his hand and smiled. 'No, nothing like that.'

12

Then her emotions seesawed. Terror gripped her again as she remembered the question she had to ask. She gripped his hand. 'Guy, tell me . . . you did buy a lottery ticket today, didn't you?' He started to fumble for his wallet. 'Just tell me!' she screeched. 'Did you?'

'Yes, of course . . .' His face drained. Now it was his turn to grip her hand, so hard her bones crunched. 'What? You don't mean?'

'Was it the usual numbers?' she snapped. Her breath came searing up through her throat in harsh gasps. 'You didn't alter them? Please God, say you didn't alter them!'

He pulled out his wallet and found the ticket. His agitated fingers crumpled it, dropped it.

'Careful!' she yelled, picking it up. She smoothed it out on the arm of the chair and stared at the computer print. The crossed-fingers logo danced before her eyes on the pink and white checkerboard. Yes, there were the familiar birthday numbers. A profound relief swept through her, followed by a whoop of elation. 'We've won, love! A third share of the bloody jackpot! We've won the lottery!'

'What?' She had never seen his eyes open so wide. 'Are you sure? Where's the numbers? Let's check them.'

Sara flicked the TV on again and sat with her arm around her husband while he checked the numbers for himself. He went very quiet. Then he said, 'God, Sara, we've really done it, haven't we?'

'YES!' She leapt from the chair, pulling him towards her. 'Show some feeling, Guy, for heaven's sake – we've won the bloody lottery!'

He still looked dazed, turning the ticket over in

his hand and squinting to try and read the small print on the back. 'I suppose we should phone them. then. Make sure it's right.'

'Of course it's right . . . !'

Sara's head was spinning, but beneath all the confusion a warning note was sounding. She was acutely aware that for her and Guy life was about to be transformed, and a fearful regret overtook her. What if this was the beginning of the end for them? What if they couldn't handle it? Their marriage, that had seemed to be on a downward slide, might quickly accelerate into ruin now.

'Wait!' She placed a restraining hand on his arm. 'Don't try ringing them yet. I need some time to . . . absorb it all. Please, Guy.'

He looked at her, his face a blank. She tried to put some of her fears into words. 'This will be the end of all our money troubles, and that's going to be fantastic. But what will happen to us, love? Will we stay the same?'

'What do you mean?'

Sara felt the vague sense of desperation within her crystallise into sudden, one-pointed desire. 'Make love to me, Guy! Let me know you still love me, then I'm sure everything will be OK. Please!'

His dark-brown eyes glinted into sharp focus. Sara recognised the old gleam of lust as his hands swept down her body to clutch at her buttocks, dragging her close. The prospect of becoming a millionaire had fuelled his libido too. With a groan she began to push up his shirt, her fingernails scratching at the warm fur on his chest as she attempted to strip him.

'Sara, we're going to be rich, babe . . .'

His whispered words rang erotically in her ear, charging her up still further. She was frantic for it now, needing the reassurance of an orgasm. Letting Guy undo his trousers, she pulled her own blouse off without bothering to undo all the buttons. Several popped off and bounced on the carpet, making her giggle. What did a few buttons matter now? She'd soon have enough to buy a whole button factory! For once in her life, she didn't have to be careful.

Still in a capricious mood she invited Guy to rip her underclothes off. Smiling, he wrenched her bra-straps from the cups and the garment began to fall from her pert breasts, hooking itself momentarily on her nipples before drifting down to her feet. His mouth seized on them hungrily, sucking at the already erect nubs so hard that she felt the sexual electricity zap down her spine and spread to her legs, making them feel wobbly.

'I have to lie down,' she murmured.

They threw down the sofa cushions and made a cosy nest for themselves on the floor. Soon Guy was kneeling beside her, his erection good and hard, and Sara felt her womb swoop with longing. She took the tip of his penis between her lips and began to nibble softly at the taut glans, making him squirm with pleasure.

'God, Sara, you know I love it when you do that!'

She felt a twinge of guilt. How long was it since she'd fellated him? Well, that didn't matter; everything was different now. As her desire gathered force Sara recognised the joy she'd felt at the beginning of their relationship, when their love was new and exciting. So it was possible to revive that early enthusiasm! Tenderly she sucked at the eye of his penis and tasted the salty juice that was starting to seep out.

Guy groaned and swung round so his head was at her groin. His fingers pulled at the flimsy lace around her hips until it snapped, giving him full access to her mound, then he invaded her gently. Sara was aware of her own flowing juices, bathing the whole of her vulva and allowing his fingers to slip easily around its tumid contours. She felt exhilaration roller-coast through her body on a nonstop adrenaline ride, and shifted her pelvis to make herself even more open to his caresses.

By the time Guy's wet mouth found her clitoris she was on the verge of coming, and it took only a few strokes of his tongue to bring her to the nerve-tingling brink. For a moment she hesitated, conscious of having to choose between the immediate satisfaction of cunnilingus and the delayed delights of intercourse.

It didn't take her long to make up her mind.

'Come inside me!' she gasped, wanting to feel him ride, hard and strong, right into the hungry heart of her sex.

Guy obliged at once, kneeling between her outspread thighs with his eager cock pink and swollen with pride. Sara guided the stiff shaft with her hand until it was lodged between her lower lips, ready to enter her. For a few seconds she let the mouth of her vagina squeeze the hard flesh, enjoying the suspense until it became unbearable and she just had to let him in. Then she held her breath until she felt its hardness slide into her, probing every inch of her pussy until the mouth of his glans gave the mouth of her womb a soft kiss.

16

She shuddered, her flesh quivering with keen sensation, her mind and body perfectly focused on the act of love.

'Oh God!' she moaned, the memory of what had initiated all this ecstasy suddenly resurfacing. 'A million, Guy! A bloody million!'

The idea of such excess seized her with voluptuous force. She could see them wallowing in sunshine by some luxurious hotel pool, making love on a secluded beach, in the back of a stretch limo. She could feel the years of fretful strife melt away into the delicious pleasure of never having to worry again. No worries. The phrase made her smile.

Her body was responding to her new mood of self-indulgent hedonism. Sara sighed as the longed-for ascent towards climax began. Her hips were moving in a lithe rhythm and her clitoris was contracting against the base of Guy's cock as it moved rapidly in and out, bringing her the sweetest pleasure. Again they were lovers, real lovers, the way they had once been.

Guy thrust harder and faster, his own climax imminent. His fingers clutched at her breasts with almost cruel force, but Sara was scarcely aware of it. Her own fingers were dug fimly into the taut mounds of his buttocks, urging him on. Their pubic bones were clashing like sword on shield, but their personal combat was to their mutual benefit, each bent on wresting every last drop of satisfaction from the body of the other.

It was a long time since they'd climaxed together, but this time they did it. Fierce waves of bliss ran like purifying fire from Sara's pelvis out through her body, making her fingers and toes tingle with delight. Her pussy was convulsing strongly, over and over, clutching at Guy's penis until she felt him give a long spurt and come with her, their bodies exchanging erotic heat, their minds and hearts linked in sensual heaven. When she returned to awareness Sara found she couldn't remember ever having such a mind-blowing climax, and from the way that Guy was moaning out the last of his passion she guessed that he must feel the same.

Overcome with tenderness, she took him in her arms. He spasmed a few more times then was still, embracing her loosely, the sweet, animal odours of his body enveloping her. Sara lay in quiet exhaustion, waiting for the full realisation of their win to hit her again. For a while she was full of wistfulness, as if their coupling had destroyed some other virginity, some intact state of being that could never be recovered once their own personal lottery ball was set rolling. She felt almost regretful, remembering good times and bad, knowing things would never be quite the same again. Fervently she hoped they could only get better.

At last she shifted Guy's head onto her lap and began to stroke his hair, bringing him gently back to her. He opened his eyes wide and grinned, his face upside down. His eyes were full of a mischievous light, as if they had stolen the prize rather than won it.

'All right,' she grinned back. 'Go on! You can phone them up now!'

Chapter Two

'*IT'S BEEN QUITE* a shock, I expect.'

The sympathetic smile of Jackie, the winners' adviser, looked as if she knew exactly what Sara and Guy were going through. Their claim had been verified at around midnight and she had arrived at noon the next day to see them through the initial stages. In her mid-thirties, well-groomed and wearing a smart blue suit, she made Sara, who had thrown on a T-shirt and jeans and was still wearing her slippers, feel very scruffy.

When they were all sitting in the front room Sara reminded her, 'On the phone you told us to do nothing and tell nobody. Why is that?'

'You might do or say something you'd later regret. It's important to take your time. You've had a complete shock – of the nicest possible kind, of course – and you can't be expected to act normally for quite some time. I mean, what used to be normal for you just isn't any more, is it?'

'What happens next?' Guy asked. His voice sounded uncharacteristically faint. 'I mean, when do we . . . you know?'

'Get the money?' Jackie gave a knowing smile. 'Tomorrow.'

'Tomorrow?'

'Yes. Most people are surprised. But once your claim has been validated there's no point in drawing it out, is there? You'll have a great deal to think about, and the sooner your plans are based on some firm foundation the better.'

Sara tried to imagine herself taking a cheque for one-point-something million along to her local bank branch. She couldn't.

Jackie seemed to read her mind. 'Of course we'll help you decide where to bank the money at first, and what to do with it later. That's the job of our financial advisers. They are there to help you as much as they can, but it's entirely up to you if you want to take advantage of their expertise. Perhaps you already have a financial adviser?'

She's fishing, Sara thought. There was no reason to be suspicious, but she could feel wariness creeping up on her. She didn't know who she wanted to tell about their win yet, if anyone. And here was this person, who meant nothing to either of them, poking her nose into their business.

'No,' Guy said, before she could stop him. 'We'll need all the help we can get, won't we Sara?'

'Mm,' she said non-committally, but her eyes flashed him a warning. He looked disoriented. But then, he'd been looking like that all night.

They hadn't slept much. After their initial exuberant lovemaking and the phone call to the regional office, they had gone to bed. Sara had wanted to make love again but Guy hadn't been up to it. He seemed completely shell-shocked and only wanted to talk. So they'd explored some of the new possibilities together.

Sara had begun, dreamily, 'We could spend the

rest of our life having holidays abroad. Two or three abroad. We could buy a villa in Spain.'

'Two villas in Spain!' Guy had grinned.

'A whole bloody Spanish village, if we want to.'

'Are we going to give any away?'

'What, to charity?'

Guy gave her a reproving look. 'No, I meant to my family, actually.'

'Oh, them!'

It was at that point that Sara decided she definitely wanted no publicity. Not yet, at least. The thought of Guy's relatives squabbling over who should get what was very distasteful. For once she was glad that she had never known her real parents. She had been taken into care as a baby and never known what it was like to have a family until she married Guy, when she found out that family life was not quite the bed of roses she'd imagined as a child. Now she regarded the prospect of telling his relatives about their good fortune with trepidation.

The Kingsleys would squabble once they heard about their win, she was sure of that. It might be best not to give anyone anything, and that meant keeping their win secret. But how could they go on a spending spree without arousing suspicion? It was all rather disturbing.

They both rang into work to say they were feeling ill. It wasn't far off the truth. Jon showed a surprising degree of concern, making Sara feel guilty, but she assured him that it was just a cold or, at worst, a bout of flu. She hated lying but, like everything else about her new life, it seemed par for the course. She suspected that she would be telling quite a few in the months to come.

21

Jackie promised to go through everything with them as many times as they needed. She said that most people needed to have things repeated because it was all too new, too distracting. Sara was glad to have her around, but she resented the fact that she was so dependent on a stranger to show her the ropes. Somehow she feared that their privacy would be at a premium from now on, even if they did manage to keep the whole thing secret.

'I'll leave you alone now,' Jackie said at last. 'You'll want to talk things over between you. But I'm staying at the George. If you need me any time, day or night, just give me a ring.'

'You sound like a Samaritan,' Guy joked.

Jackie gave him another of her knowing looks, but smiled as she took her leave.

The minute she was out of the house Sara pulled Guy into her arms. 'Let's go upstairs,' she whispered. 'I want us to celebrate in our own way – you know how!'

There was an itch that needed scratching, and it was more than just physical. Sara needed the reassurance of his loving, to assuage the weird feelings that were irritating her inside. She should have been over the moon, one hundred per cent happy. Why on earth wasn't she?

'I don't know if I can manage anything,' Guy warned.

'Don't worry,' Sara grinned. 'I'll do all the work!'

She could feel the hot pulse between her thighs, making her heart race, making her wet. As soon as they got into the bedroom she pulled her husband's T-shirt over his head and ran her hands over his warm chest. She slipped his belt through the buckle

22

and unzipped his jeans, then crossed her arms in front of her chest and pulled off the T-shirt she'd slipped on that morning. She wore no bra, and her breasts were full and heavy, the ripening nipples firming even more on exposure to the air until they protruded with tingling stiffness.

'Lie down!' she told Guy, once he had taken off his trousers. His pants showed the beginning of an erection, something to work on. She began to knead his cock softly through the loose cotton and he gave a groan in response. Soon she was straddling him. 'Lick my tits, Guy! Make me feel like a million dollars.'

He laughed rather self-consciously, and she saw a flame of excitement flicker in his dark-brown eyes. Poor thing, she thought. He seemed even more overwhelmed than she was. She longed for him to let go of the shock, the fear, the superstitious belief that he didn't deserve it. She wanted him to begin to enjoy the prospect of all that money, all that freedom. Until he did, it was impossible for her to fully experience those positive feelings herself. Slowly his open mouth approached her swaying breasts, fastened on a nipple and began to suck. Sara felt her insides contract with heightened desire and she began to squeeze his cock more purposefully through his cotton boxer shorts. It began to firm up to most satisfactory dimensions, and Guy's mouth suckled harder as his excitement grew. She lifted the waistband of his shorts and the tumid glans thrust itself into her hand, seeking stimulation.

'Oh God, we can do anything we want now!' Sara murmured, the realisation hitting her anew for the umpteenth time.

But then came a wicked murmur in her head: And *have* anyone we want, too?

Sara ignored the siren voice, bending down her head to give Guy's now-rampant penis a tonguing. Already the glans was becoming salty with his juice, so she would have to go carefully. It would be a disaster if he came before she could get him inside her. She gave his shaft a last, loving sweep with her tongue then positioned herself so that she could slide his glans into her entrance.

For a while she squeezed him, making the ring of muscle clutch repeatedly at his rock-hard erection, enjoying the rapid fluttering in her vagina that was prelude to the satisfaction of having him fill her up. When she could bear the suspense no longer she began to inch down on him, her vaginal muscles still working rhythmically, milking mutual pleasure from the rigid organ. She wiggled and thrust her hips to wrest every nuance of delight from the contact, the nerves in her clitoris zinging with excitement as she propelled herself closer to orgasm.

Through the blurred haze of her consciousness Sara was thinking. Over a fucking million! We're going to be millionaires, for God's sake! Then her mind began to open up with possibilities, turning their lovemaking into a fantasy fuck. Except now things were different. She could dream of making love on exotic beaches and in luxurious hotel rooms all she liked, but whereas only yesterday they would have been wild dreams, now they were wishes that could easily be fulfilled.

Sara pictured a warm, deserted beach with the soothing sound of lapping waves and the distant cries of birds. The sand would be pale and virgin, the vegetation that fringed it lush and shady. The body that lay so welcomingly outstretched would be tanned and muscular, perfectly proportioned. She tried to turn it into Guy's body but somehow the metamorphosis just wouldn't take place. The eager lover with the finely honed physique and the large, thick penis was also possessed of a film-star face, and no amount of trying could superimpose her husband's familiar features on that make-believe hunk.

Giving up the struggle with a sigh, Sara sank into the fantasy and let it take her where she wanted to go. For months this had been the pattern on the rare occasions when they made love: she could only come if she pretended that she was making love to a stranger. Of course she felt guilty about it, but she reasoned that it was better to do it that way than not at all. At least Guy got his rocks off too.

The dream lover was crooning softly at her, 'You're so-o-o beautiful, babe!' while he swivelled his pelvis in a sensual horizontal dance, making his thick rod move around like a spoon, stirring the mixture of warm flesh and sticky juices that was her vagina. That million dollar feeling was dawning in her soul, lifting the whole experience onto the plane of the miraculous. The hot throb of her clitoris was driving her now, her sexual excitement almost matching the thrill of winning. Somehow they merged in her psyche, so that she felt as if she were about to gain the whole world. A huge thrill of exhilaration shuddered through her, almost as intense as an orgasm but not quite. The sensation of richness was filling her senses, making her feel so much more alive.

His cock was like a golden finger deep inside, stroking her tenderly while his lips and tongue poured warm honey over her nipples. He was in love with her, this handsome stranger; he'd do anything to please her. Sara pictured sliding off his erection for a few minutes while he licked her pussy, something that Guy would do only rarely and reluctantly. Her imagination transformed his penis into a warm, agile tongue that knew exactly how to make the kind of delicate strokes that nudged her clitoris towards ecstasy.

Sara was on the brink and she badly wanted to come, but something was holding her back. She felt guilty. The knowledge that Guy had become depersonalised, that he was no longer her desired husband but just a token male, a convenient penis, was making her ashamed. She growled out her frustration and resurrected the image of the anonymous lover. He was entering her from behind now – ah, that was better! – clutching at her swinging breasts from behind while he drove into her with all the might of a pile-driver.

The climax that had been evading her now began to break – like a glorious sunrise, filling her body with the welcome spasms of release. Moaning in bliss, Sara fell forward onto her husband's prostrate body, which in her fantasy became hot sand. His penis twitched inside, needing more stimulation before it could find the satisfaction it craved. But, for the time being, Sara was locked in her own private heaven and could do no more for him.

She rolled off and onto the bed, utterly satiated, and Guy took her in his arms. His stroking of her breasts and nibbling kisses irritated her now, and she shrugged him off.

'Come on, fair's fair,' he moaned. 'Help me to get off too, for goodness' sake!'

Half-heartedly she tugged at his erect cock until he became annoyed and pushed her hand away. 'I'll do it myself,' he muttered.

'Sorry, love, I'm exhausted. Hardly slept last night.'

'Not too tired to have one yourself though,' she heard him mutter, before she turned on her side and fell into a doze.

Next day, Jackie drove them to the regional office, judging correctly that neither of them was in a fit state to sit behind a driving wheel. The cheque was handed over with minimal ceremony, seeing as they'd specified no publicity. It was made out to both of them so they opened a joint account there and then. The gold credit card was an unexpected bonus.

'What will you do now?' Jackie asked, when the formalities were over. 'Most people like to have a celebratory meal somewhere special.'

Sara had been thinking about it. 'First, I'd like to go to the best beauty salon in town and have a top-to-toe job. Then I want to go into all those dress shops I've never been in because I knew they'd be too expensive. I'm going to shop till I drop!'

'A nice meal,' Guy repeated thoughtfully. 'I reckon I could do justice to a juicy steak now. I haven't been able to eat a thing yet. I brought my breakfast straight up.'

'That's only to be expected,' Jackie smiled understandingly. 'Would you like me to book you both a table for tonight?'

'Somewhere really expensive – but exclusive,

too,' Sara added. 'Somewhere even *Hello!* magazine hasn't heard of.'

Jackie nodded. 'I know just the place – you'll love it. Shall we say eight o'clock?'

'Would you like to join us?' Guy asked, making Sara's heart sink. 'You've been so kind, seeing us through all this.'

Her reply made Sara's heart lift again. 'Oh no, I think it's better for you to be by yourselves tonight. You have another long day tomorrow, if you're going to see our financial team. Not that you need to do anything like that yet, of course. Only when you feel up to it.'

After ringing around on Sara's behalf, Jackie announced that she would have to make do with the third-best beauty salon in town. The other two were booked up with regular clients for weeks ahead. It was Sara's first intimation that she was a newcomer, not yet accepted into the charmed circle of big spenders. Perhaps she never would be.

'While you're there, I'll pop along to that bespoke shoemaker's on Wymark Street,' Guy said. 'Always fancied having my shoes handmade. I'll order a made-to-measure suit or two as well.'

Sara felt a sudden, acute pang of regret. She remembered that their last row had been about him buying a suit. The fact that they would never argue over money again should have made her happy but, strangely, it didn't.

Jackie called them a taxi. Even though she was being very sweet, very efficient, and Sara didn't know what she would have done without her, the woman was getting on her nerves. It wasn't her fault, or the lottery people's. Everyone had her best interests at heart, hers and Guy's. But she needed time to assimilate it all, time by herself. She was looking forward to relaxing in that beauty salon.

Being pampered was something that didn't happen to Sara very often. As she wallowed in the steam room, prior to having her pores cleansed, she looked round at the other pampered ladies and felt a shiver of delight run through her. These were all wealthy women. Even though they were clad in identical pink towels, their carefully shaped brows, manicured nails and firm flesh proclaimed that they had the best physical care money could buy lavished upon them.

She smiled nervously at the blonde woman nearest her. 'I've not seen you in here before, have I?' the woman said with a confident smile. Sara shook her head. 'It's a marvellous place to unwind. In town for the shopping, are you?'

Without revealing too much, Sara managed to convey that she was new to the area and could do with some advice about where to find the best boutiques. The woman, who introduced herself as Katerina, was generous with her tips. By the time Sara emerged from the salon, with her dark-blonde hair lightened a couple of shades and twisted into a sophisticated knot and her perfectly made-up face gleaming with health, she had her diary filled with fashionable names and addresses. It was a relief to have something to do, she decided, as she boldly hailed a taxi and gave the first of several smart names to the driver.

At seven she was meeting Guy in a fashionable bar. When she walked in she saw him at once, conspicuous in a light-grey off-the-peg suit that was nevertheless very well cut. The pale lilac shirt and rather jazzy tie gave him the look of a city whizz kid, and had the unexpected effect of making her heart skip a beat.

He didn't recognise her, though. Sara smiled as she walked towards him, saw him glance at her, look away again and then back, recognition only slowly dawning.

'Sara, it *is* you! My God, you look fantastic! I love your hair.'

She did a twirl to show off her slinky jersey wool dress with the matching jacket. The cornflower blue of the outfit highlighted her eyes and the expert make-up gave her an understated model-girl look that took years off her.

'We both look fantastic,' she conceded. 'Amazing what money can do, isn't it? Maybe I'll have my tits done.'

'Don't you dare!' He kissed her cheek possessively. 'I like them just the way they are. Mind you, I wouldn't object to you having a thigh job.'

She punched him playfully, laughter welling up in her like champagne bubbles. It was ages since they'd had such fun, smiled and joked so much. Perhaps it was just beginning to sink in and they were starting to enjoy their new-found wealth at last.

Despite their nervousness at being in such an obviously smart restaurant as Carmino's, Sara and Guy enjoyed their exquisitely cooked and presented meal. The atmosphere of quiet reverence in which the food was served overawed them at first, but soon Sara was relishing the discreet peace of the place. After the whirlwind events of the day it was nice to chat quietly over a bottle of fine wine, with an attentive waiter hovering in the background.

'You know, I've been thinking about my family,' Guy began, when they were onto dessert. He sucked some light-as-a-feather chocolate soufflé off his spoon. 'I really don't think I can hide this from them, Sara. I've always told them everything.'

'If you tell them, you'll have to share the money with them.' Sara frowned.

His dark eyes penetrated hers and his mouth took on the slightly petulant shape that she knew meant business. 'Is that such a bad thing? I'd like to help them, Mark and Penny at least. I don't know about Mum.'

'Well there you are, major stumbling block number one. You can hardly tell your brother and sister but not your mother. And you know how she feels about gambling. She's lectured you on the subject often enough.'

Guy's father had been an inveterate gambler before he died, and had left the family in quite a bit of debt. The irony was that, although even a tiny fraction of their lottery win would pay off those debts, Anne Kingsley would probably be too proud, and too indignant, to accept it.

'I can't help it, Sara, I must offer. I'd never be able to live with myself if I didn't.'

Sara's chocolate soufflé turned to mud in her mouth as she contemplated what this might mean. If he told his relatives, they would be sure to quarrel over their share of the million. She could see the sum dwindling. But then a possible solution struck her. 'OK, suppose we tell them only half the truth.'

'What do you mean?'

'Well we don't have to say we've won a million, do we? We can pretend we won one of the lower

31

prizes – five balls, maybe. Then they won't expect so much from us.'

It seemed the perfect solution to her, but Guy was unconvinced. 'They might find out.'

'How? Do you suppose they'd check up on us? We did say no publicity, remember.'

'Hm. D'you remember how much the other prizes were?'

'I think five balls plus bonus was four hundred thousand and something. Five balls was around sixty thousand. We can check on Teletext.'

'I'd feel terrible saying it was only sixty thousand.'

'Say four hundred thousand then. It's a big enough sum for them not to be surprised if we buy a new house or a car, or go on holiday.'

'I'd feel mean.'

'For goodness' sake, Guy, there's no need to feel guilty about this, you know! It could have been any one of them winning. And do you think they'd have given you much of their prize money?'

He shrugged, looking miserable. Sara squeezed his hand. 'Four hundred thousand-odd it is, then. We'd better decide which of the six balls to leave out, and we'd better get the exact sum right, too.'

Guy grimaced. 'You make it sound like a conspiracy.'

'It's for the best, love. We'll give them whatever you want. What do you think, fifty thousand each?'

'Out of four hundred thousand? That's a bit much.'

Sara began to laugh hysterically, almost choking on the rich soufflé that she had just spooned into her mouth. 'God, Guy, you are just amazing! A minute ago you were wanting to share a chunk of a million with them, and now you say fifty thousand is too much!'

'I only meant, if we're going to tell them a white lie we may as well make it convincing,' he said sulkily. 'OK, let's say twenty thousand each. That'll help Mark get a new car and maybe pay off some of his mortgage. And Penny can pay off her student loan. I know that's been worrying her.'

'What about your mother?'

'We'll cross that bridge when we come to it! Let's not talk about money any more though, Sara – not tonight. I've had it about up to here.'

'Me, too. What's the name of the hotel we're staying at? Let's get the waiter to order us a taxi and pay the bill. I can't wait to get to bed.' She grinned mischievously. 'And I don't mean to sleep.'

The hotel was small, elegant and very comfortable: not too overpowering or fussy. Sara and Guy took a brandy up to their room which had a luxurious bathroom, thick carpet everywhere and a king-size bed. As soon as the door was closed she put down her brandy glass on the Regency-style bedside table, kicked off her smart new high heels and flopped down on the springy mattress.

'Oh, this is bliss!' she exclaimed. 'I want a long soak in a hot bath. None of your stand-up showers for me. Then I want you to take me to bed and make long, slow love to me. All that, combined with the brandy, should get me to sleep tonight, if nothing else will.'

'I'll wash your back.' Guy grinned.

It was almost like the old days, Sara decided, as she wallowed with closed eyes in the scented foam. Her limbs felt languid, her breasts were being gently roused by her husband's soapy fingers and, for the first time in ages, she began to feel totally relaxed. She could feel the softness of her sex unfolding beneath the water, her clitoris swelling with arousal, and the prospect of making love was wonderful.

Yet the minute she opened her eyes and saw Guy's familiar face, her mood altered to one of vague irritation. Something was niggling at her, but she didn't quite know what. Was it to do with him wanting to tell his family? Or was it something deeper than that? Sighing, she closed her eyes again and was soon luxuriating in sensuality. She thought about being rich. It still hadn't quite sunk in. Sometimes she caught herself thinking about work, or about paying the bills, just like the old days. And they were very much the old days now. Her life before the lottery win almost seemed to belong to someone else.

'Come on, let me dry you,' she heard Guy say.

Roused from her voluptuous musing, Sara had to quell another of those brief pangs of annoyance as she stepped into the huge fluffy bath sheet. When he had towelled her, Guy led her into the bedroom, where he proceeded to apply a luxurious scented lotion to her warm, soft body. Passively Sara lapped up the attention, her breasts now full and straining while her nipples crested them like alert watchtowers.

Sensing her need, Guy dipped one creamy forefinger between her labia to find the slippery nub and began to stimulate her in earnest. With his other hand he tweaked both her nipples in turn then flicked his fingers across them teasingly while he continued to caress her down below, the arousal of both her erogenous hot spots making her pussy shudder with longing.

'Come for me, baby!' he whispered, but his voice sounded alien to her ears. He never normally spoke to her like that. Was he striving to live out some fantasy of being a playboy lover?

She arched her back and thrust her pelvis harder against his hand, seeking more stimulation. He took the cue and slowly thrust his finger inside her. She clamped his finger and he moaned aloud, evidently imagining how it would feel to have her seize his cock with her vaginal walls like that. Outside she was all wet and slippery, her clitoris bulging against his wrist so that every time he moved his hand in and out of her, the tingling throb of her approaching orgasm intensified.

Only by transforming her lover into a faceless hunk could Sara bring herself to roll over the brink into complete sexual satisfaction. She was soon back with her handsome beach boy; the cream that Guy was still rubbing into her breasts and stomach was transformed into suntan cream, and she was on some hot, exotic shore with nothing to do but lead a hedonistic lifestyle. The fact that this dream was now well within her reach added piquancy to the fantasy and it didn't take her long to slide over the edge into blissful oblivion, her whole body reverberating to the pulsing rhythm of a mind-shattering climax.

When she recovered, Sara found herself being cradled in her husband's arms. He had pulled back the white silken quilt and she found herself on satin sheets, cool and pristine beneath her sweaty body. Smiling, she smoothed a hand over the crisp frills of the pillow.

'Luxury,' she murmured. 'We're going to spend the rest of our lives in the lap of luxury. Who'd have believed it, a week ago?'

'A week ago,' Guy murmured in wonder, remembering. They were both struck dumb by the enormity of it. Such a total transformation of their lives, and in so few days!

'I'm ... er ... very tired,' Guy said at last. 'Do you mind if I turn out the light?'

Sara said she didn't, but she had to admit to herself that she was disappointed. She'd hoped for a long, sensual session and felt only just primed for it, but now it would have to be postponed. Still, now she came to think of it, she was exhausted too. There would be plenty of opportunity for them to make love again. After all, they could spend whole days in hotel beds anywhere in the world, now.

So why didn't the prospect of such a lifestyle make her happy? While Guy began to snore beside her, Sara stared at the ceiling where flickering lights from the outside world were faintly projected. It seemed a kind of omen, as if 'real life' might become just a distant show for them now, without any true meaning. The idea alarmed her. Maybe they should give away most of their new-found wealth to good causes. And then there was the question of Guy's family. Thank God she didn't have any relatives of her own. For the first time in her life, she felt quite relieved that her mother had abandoned her when she was a baby.

This is ridiculous, Sara told herself as she rolled over to sleep. She vowed there and then that she would enjoy her money, not think of it as a problem. If she did encounter any problem along the way, there was nothing that couldn't be solved if you threw enough money at it, and now she could do just that. A holiday, that was what she and Guy needed most, and as soon as possible. Turning her mind to the pleasant prospect of choosing where in the world she wanted to go, Sara soon drifted into sweet dreams.

Chapter Three

TELLING GUY'S FAMILY about their win proved to be just the mistake that Sara had thought it would be. He chickened out of revealing the exact sum so it was left to her to repeat the figure for the five balls score: four hundred and three thousand, two hundred and fifty-five pounds. She almost choked saying it, but then Guy broke in to say that he was giving his brother and sister twenty thousand each and their faces were suddenly transformed from shocked incredulity to joy.

'I'll be able to pay off my loan,' Penny grinned, throwing her arms around him. 'Thanks a million, big brother!'

At least Guy had the grace to blush.

'What about Mum?' Mark asked, after issuing his gruff thanks. 'Do you want us to tell her?'

Guy's mother was convalescing after a hernia operation. 'Not yet,' Guy said. 'I don't want to upset her, especially while she's recovering.'

'She won't approve,' Penny said. 'You know how she feels about gambling. She's always sounding off about the lottery. Says it's turning us into a nation of gamblers.'

'Mm, I know. Maybe it's best to say nothing at all.'

'Well I don't know about you,' Mark grinned, 'but I intend to go in for a bit of conspicuous consumption. I already had my eye on a second-hand Jag. Now I'll be able to afford it. But how will I explain it to Mum?'

Sara butted in. 'That's hardly our concern, is it, Mark?'

'Well, it should be. Come to that, how are you going to explain any extravagances you go in for? I'm sure you won't be leaving all your winnings in the bank, now will you?'

His sneering tone hinted that he regarded Sara as a bit of a spendthrift. This attitude had angered her in the past, particularly as it was generally Guy who squandered their hard-earned cash. She scowled at Mark, but knew he did have a point. The Kingsley family lived in fear of their autocratic mama, who would definitely disapprove if she found out about their win. And what she would say if she knew the full extent of the prize money didn't bear thinking about.

'I think we should all agree on whether to tell Anne or not,' she said coolly. 'Then we'll all have to accept the consequences of that decision.'

'I'm in favour of keeping it secret,' Penny said at once.

'But then I'd have to lie, say I've got a rise at work or something,' Mark objected.

'It wouldn't be the first time you've lied to mother, would it?' Guy said.

'What exactly do you mean by that remark?'

It looked as if the two brothers were spoiling for a fight. Sara did her best to defuse the situation.

'Look, let's try to be civilised about this, shall we? We've had some good luck, for heaven's sake, and we want to share it with you both. We should be toasting each other in champagne, not squabbling.'

'I'd like to buy Ma a new house, if she'd let me,' Guy said, dolefully. 'But I'm sure she wouldn't.'

Penny turned to Sara. 'Couldn't you dream up some long-lost relative, say they've died and left you a small fortune?'

'Hey, that's a good idea.' Guy grinned.

'But she knows I don't have any relatives.'

'You could say you had a call from a lawyer saying your long-lost uncle left you all his money because he had no children.' Guy put his arm around her and kissed her on the cheek. She recognised it as a placatory gesture because she often got upset when she thought about her family – or lack of one.

'Oh, tell her what you like,' she said wearily. 'I'll just go along with it, like I always do.'

It made her sick, the way Guy's family behaved. Having none of her own, Sara often wondered why they quarrelled and fussed over everything. Why couldn't they just be grateful they had each other? Now the idea of dreaming up some long-forgotten relative of hers seemed faintly ridiculous, but she could think of no better plan.

A week later Sara and Guy visited Anne Kingsley and told her the news. She received it non-committally, which was the best they could have hoped for, and resolutely refused Guy's offer of financial help, as he'd known she would.

'I've always managed,' she said, tight-lipped. 'But now it means I can spend more of my savings on myself without having to worry about you two.'

So it seemed a reasonable compromise. But then came the phone calls from the rest of the family. Mark told them that his dream Jag was a bit knackered and would need more money spent on it to make it roadworthy. The total cost would be a little over the twenty thousand, so did they think they could see their way to lending him another five?

Sara was incensed. 'The cheek of it! Talk about looking a gift-horse in the mouth. If he can't afford that car, he should look for another. There must be plenty of second-hand Jaguars on the market if you know where to go.'

Guy wanted to lend him the extra but she told him he was being a fool and, in the end, he shame-facedly refused his brother. Relations soured between them. Then Penny phoned and said she was afraid that Mark might tell their mother the truth, out of pique. Sara bit back the urge to say, 'I told you so,' and instead suggested to Guy that they should go on holiday until things blew over.

'I've had it up to here with your family,' she sighed. 'All I want is the chance to relax for a week or two and enjoy our winnings.'

He agreed at once. 'OK. Where would you like to go?'

Sara's mind flipped back to the film she'd been watching before she decided to check the lottery numbers. It seemed half a lifetime ago, yet the images of the beautiful Californian coastline were still vivid. 'California,' she declared. 'I wouldn't mind hiring a beach apartment somewhere around L.A. Malibu would be nice.'

'Are you joking? That would cost—' Guy caught himself in time, threw back his head and gave a great roar of laughter. 'Sure, baby,' he said, in a

41

fake American accent. 'Anything you want, doll. The sky's the limit, now we got mega-bucks!'

It took a little while to find the holiday home of their dreams through an exclusive agency that Jackie recommended. They decided to fly to New York, take a look around for a couple of days, then go on to L.A.

Meanwhile, Sara rang Jon to tell him she was exhausted and would like to take the rest of her annual leave, while Guy rang his boss and told him the same tale. They had both decided to put their careers on hold rather than resign and risk regretting it later. Sara wasn't sure how much of her life she wanted to change. It had all happened so suddenly, with scarcely any time to draw breath, and now she wanted to be far away from it all to help her get things into perspective. It still hadn't sunk in completely. She found herself worrying vaguely about paying the bills or wondering whether she could afford something, and then had to remind herself that she needn't think that way any more. It was marvellous to have such freedom!

Neither of them had been to America before and New York was a wonderland, but it took them a couple of days to recover from jet lag. After walking for miles around Manhattan, taking in everything from Rockefeller Plaza to Central Park, they flopped into their hotel bed each night and fell asleep without making love. Sara was disappointed, but she told herself that once they were installed in their glorified beach hut at Malibu they could start living their dream.

The flight across the continent seemed interminable but at last they arrived at Los Angeles airport, where they took a cab. Soon they were being whisked along the freeway to Sunset Boulevard, past miles of sprawling suburbs to the ocean. Malibu, far from being the arty seaside village of Sara's imagination, was a great sprawling suburb with a main road that wound all along the backs of the houses. They were a mixed lot too, many obviously luxurious but others that seemed quite run-down and little more than ramshackle. Sara grew anxious as the driver did his best to locate Mariposa Villa. Booking at such a distance had been a gamble, even though the agency had seemed very upmarket. What if their luxury holiday home turned out to be little more than a shack?

She needn't have worried. When the driver drew up at the back of the villa, a high wall covered with purple bougainvillea gave the place a chic, almost continental air. Beyond the high wall, Sara glimpsed a balcony with more trailing plants and shuttered windows, gleaming with fresh green paint. Guy tipped the cabbie generously then found the door key on the ring of three they'd been given, together with the combination for the security panel. Soon the pair of them were inside the wall and staring, goggle-eyed, at what they saw around them.

The courtyard was filled with Italian-style statuary and a little fountain that played from the mouth of a cupid. There was a swing lounger, and a staircase to the upper level with a brightly coloured pot plant on each step. At ground level there was a patio door which Guy opened with another of the keys, letting them into a small but expensively furnished room decorated in pastel colours.

A breakfast bar stood in one corner and there was a home-cinema in another. A huge settee in bright pink and pale green stretched almost the length of one wall. They walked across the thick carpet into a tiny modern kitchen that was equipped with everything they could need, including a well-stocked fridge whose door was groaning with cans of beer and bottles of Californian wine.

'Wow, this is heaven!' Sara exclaimed. 'Let's put a pizza in the microwave and toss some of this dressing on that gorgeous salad. I'm starving.'

While the pizza cooked they went upstairs and gasped as they drew up the blinds. The front of the villa faced the Pacific, and since they had arrived at sunset the view from the balcony outside the window was glorious. Directly below was a small pool, with lights already gleaming on the turquoise water. There was carefully tended grass around it and a paved patio, with table and chairs surrounded by exotic potted plants. Beyond was thick vegetation, screening the house and garden from the beach. They had already been told that the beach directly in front of the villa was private, for use of the residents only. Against the deepening blue sky the tops of palm trees waved in the evening breeze.

'Oh, it's so beautiful,' Sara exclaimed. 'Let's eat our pizza out there, shall we?'

Minutes later, they were sprawled on the loungers by the pool, swilling down the scorching hot food with ice-cold beer. 'Now I really do feel like a millionaire.' Sara laughed.

Guy reached out and took her hand. 'Me too. Isn't this amazing?'

He began to caress her fingers, sending tiny prickles of delight up her arm and down her spine. Although Sara was tired, she wasn't sleepy. The stimulating effect of the beer and food had made her alert and soon she was definitely feeling randy. She smiled at her husband and slipped off her sandals. Then she got up and went over to the pool, where she dipped a toe in the water.

'It's warm,' she exclaimed, undoing the buttons of her dress. Soon she was out of it, and then dropped her undies in a heap on the grass. The slight chill in the air made her shiver as she stood poised at the tiled edge. Then Guy came up behind her and pushed her in. She gasped at the shock but was soon swimming round and round, exulting in the exercise. When she returned to where Guy was she suddenly put out her hand and grabbed him by the ankle, making him topple, fully dressed, into the pool beside her.

'Bitch!' he spluttered, reaching for the side. He got out and stripped. Sara had just a tantalising glimpse of his pale cock and balls before he dived in and caught her round the waist. 'You're going to pay for this, woman!'

'How?' she challenged him.

'Wait and see.'

A dark excitement ran through her veins at the thought of the delayed punishment. In the good old days, when they'd been keen to explore their mutual sexuality, they had sometimes indulged in mild punishment games. Was that what he wanted to do now?

While they swam round and round the blood-warm pool, the purple, pink and gold display fanned out over the horizon and then gave way to an indigo sky dotted with silver. Sara felt her heart melt, as well as her pussy. She longed for romance, as well as sex. Guy and she had once been so wonderfully in love; surely they could resurrect that old magic again? She planted her feet down and rose from the water until she was standing waist-high, with her wet hair streaking down her neck to her shoulders.

'Come here,' she whispered hoarsely to her husband.

He waded towards her, his smile shadowy and his eyes gleaming like some nocturnal creature's in the dusk. Sara felt her womb take a downward dive; the familiar tug of desire almost knocked her off her feet, it was so strong. She opened her arms to him, expecting to fall into his embrace, but instead he scooped her up with one arm around her waist and the other beneath her knees, lifting her bodily out of the water and plonking her onto the surrounding grass before climbing out of the pool himself.

Sara shivered under the cold stars, but he lifted her again and strode towards the patio. She clung to his wet, naked body, slippery as a fish in his arms, shuddering as the night-chill reached her bones.

'Don't worry, I'll soon have you warmed up,' he said gruffly, as he slid the patio door wide open with his foot then took her inside. None too gently, he deposited her on the huge sofa while he went off to the bathroom in search of towels.

Sara found the control panel for the heating and air conditioning. She notched up the temperature and soon the villa was like a warm spring day. By the time Guy returned with a luxury fluffy bath towel she was luxuriating on the sofa like a cat on heat.

'You were a very naughty girl, throwing me in the pool like that,' he chided her, as he rubbed her naked body with the towel. 'I'm still jet-lagged. I might have drowned.'

Sara giggled. 'So what are you going to do to me?'

'Put you across my knee, of course.'

He wore a velour bath robe that he had found upstairs, but it was open and she could see his penis rising solidly from the dark mat of fur below his pale stomach. This game had always turned him on in the early days of their marriage, and now it looked as though he was going to be enjoying it again – almost as much as she was.

But it was a game that had to be played in earnest. Sara pretended to shrink from the threat of corporal punishment. She cowered at the far end of the long sofa, squealing, 'No, oh, please don't do that to me!'

His hand snaked out and caught her wrist, pulling her close. 'Oh, but I must. If you're not punished, you might misbehave again.'

'What if I promise not to?'

'You may promise all you like, but first you must take your punishment for what you've already done.'

'No, please!'

She struggled to free herself, but his grip only tightened and his eyes glinted at her with cruel amusement. Although she told herself that it was only a game, Sara remembered all the times she'd nagged and shouted at him over his spendthrift ways and a real fear crept up on her. Was he about to turn this into an act of vengeance?

'Let me go!' she cried again, making a determined effort to free herself. Instinct told her this was not the same Guy she'd once loved and trusted; neither was the game they were playing entirely good clean fun. She'd sensed a tension in him ever since the night of their lottery win and knew it was about to be released in a way that frightened her.

'You won't escape me,' he said in that same gruff voice. Swiftly he pulled the belt from the robe and lashed it tightly around her wrists, securing it with a clumsy, but nonetheless tight knot. 'That should stop your tricks,' he added with a snarl.

Sara's heart was thudding loudly as she tried to get up from the sofa. Without the use of her hands to steady her she collapsed at once and fell onto the soft carpet. Guy gave a nasty laugh and snatched at the curtain-tie which he bound around her feet, effectively immobilising her. 'That's better,' he sneered. 'And if you make too much noise I'll find something for your big mouth, too.'

The thought of being gagged horrified Sara even more than her shackled limbs. She subsided into a sullen muteness, glaring at him while he sat squarely on the sofa and placed a cushion carefully over his lap, hiding his erection.

'Crawl over here,' he commanded her. 'I want to see you on your hands and knees, with your tits and arse wobbling as you move. Then I'm going to make your bottom wobble a lot more.'

Sara was about to call him all the names under the sun, but she bit her tongue just in time. Slowly she manoeuvred across the thick carpet on all fours, wondering just why she was taking all this. It was as if she had lapsed into a weird dream that she couldn't wake from. She kept telling herself that she was trying to revive her marriage, that she wanted their life to be fun now they'd won the lottery, but the niggling dread remained.

'Over my knee!' Guy snapped. She raised herself up on her knees then flopped forward over the cushion. 'Bit further forward, I want to see your tits dangling.'

Sara obeyed, her mons thrusting hard against the side of his knee with the cushion under her midriff. She could only guess at how his cock was responding. Guy began to caress her bare buttocks in a circling motion with the flat of his hand, readying them for discipline. Between her clenched thighs Sara could feel the rapid pulse of her clitoris, monitoring her excitement, but she knew that her arousal owed as much to fear as it did to desire.

'So smooth,' she heard Guy murmur. Then the first sharp tap came. The hot globes of her buttocks shuddered with the impact but it did little more than increase Sara's already rampant libido. The frisson of fear was only making her wetter, and already she could feel hot juice beginning to seep down between her thighs. She pressed her mound closer to Guy's bony knee with a faint moan and soon he struck again, this time the flat of his hand making a resounding smack, first on her right buttock then again on her left.

'Wicked girl,' he snarled in her ear. 'I'll teach you to give me a wetting like that.'

He's certainly giving me a wetting, she thought

wryly, bracing herself for the next slap. When it came, with stinging force, she began to grind her delta against the side of his knee, stimulating herself where it had most effect. She could feel her swollen labia throbbing as her clitoris thrust aggressively between her lower lips, craving fulfilment.

Now Guy was beating her in a regular rhythm, getting into the swing of it. Her buttocks were sore and smarting but she dared not beg him to end the punishment. With every enforced thud of her pelvis against his bent knees she could feel her climax approaching and there was no way she wanted him to stop now.

But he did stop, quite suddenly, leaving her dangling on the edge of disappointment. Sara remained in a kneeling position, wondering what he would do next, but she was quite unprepared for what followed. Pushing her thighs apart, he groped between them until his finger could gain access to her soaking wet pussy. Then he parted her buttocks with one hand while he thrust his finger into her virginal anus with the other, stretching it painfully.

'Ouch!' she cried, unable to help herself.

He said nothing but continued to bore into her with his thick finger, making her squirm. When the first shock was over Sara found herself beginning to accommodate him, but no sooner had she got used to the intrusion and started to find the sensations pleasurable than he introduced a second finger and a third.

'Ow, that hurts!' she exclaimed, expecting him to withdraw, but he only continued his corkscrew action.

Then his voice came at her ear again, low and insidious. 'You like this, don't you? Go on, admit it. You've always wanted it in the arse, haven't you?'

No,' she began, but beneath the pain a dark sensuality was dawning. She couldn't deny that there was something exciting about it, but the trouble was she hated the way Guy was forcing it upon her. If he would only be more gentle.

'I want you to take my cock in there,' he told her. 'Maybe not today, but sometime soon. Today I want your cunt.'

Sara gasped as he rapidly untied her feet and thrust her legs apart, entering her immediately from behind. She had never felt him so hard and rigid, never known him to take her so ruthlessly, and a part of her despised herself for giving in to him. Yet another part exulted in it.

'Things are going to be different now,' he gasped, pounding away at her until the delicate tissues felt raw and battered. 'We're equal, for the first time since we got married. There's no way you can get at me over money or anything else. We're equal, the way a man and woman should be, do you hear?'

'If we're so damn equal, how come you're treating me like a piece of meat?' Sara mumbled.

'What's that?'

She was scared of him now, too scared to repeat it. 'Nothing.'

'I think you like a bit of rough treatment; you're responding really well,' he told her, triumphantly. 'That's been my trouble all along: I've been pussy-whipped by you. Well, this is the end of all that nonsense . . . Oh God, I'm going to come!'

Sara didn't want to join him but the keen stimulation she was getting from his rough handling was pushing her closer to the edge with every stroke. Her orgasm, when it came, was almost painful in its intensity and brought her no real satisfaction. Instead she felt anger well up, even before the last erotic flutterings had ceased. How dare he treat her like that?

But now something had broken in her and she felt cowed. Wearily she collapsed onto the soft carpet and he pulled out of her, going straight up to the bathroom where she heard him running the shower. Sara lay in a desolate heap, her emotions in turmoil. Her husband had turned into some kind of strange beast overnight and she had no idea why. All she knew was that he must have been storing up grudges against her for ages and the shock of winning all that money had released his pent-up aggression.

Predictably he was contrite afterwards, bringing out the old 'I don't know what came over me' cliché. Sara felt extremely weary, as well as sore, and was in no mood for a postmortem so she had a healing soak in the whirlpool bath and then flopped into the king-size bed beside her husband.

Although Guy was soon snoring, Sara lay awake, puzzling over what had happened. Did he resent the fact that he was still with her, even though he now had enough money to pull a younger woman? He had made a great show of ogling attractive young girls in New York, boasting that he could pull any of them now he had money. If that was his attitude, their marriage couldn't last long. Whatever the reason for his extraordinary display of male dominance, it didn't augur well for their relationship.

When Sara awoke next day, the bright Californian sunshine was streaming in through the cracks and round the edges of the blinds. She stretched luxuriously in the big bed and soon realised that she was its only occupant. Blinking, she called, 'Guy?' but there was no response. She got up and pulled on a silky robe, then searched the small house. There was a note next to the coffee-maker: *Gone for a walk.*

'You might have waited for me,' she grumbled.

Sara made coffee and had some of the delicious fruit salad and yoghurt from the fridge, then she got dressed in white shorts and a blue cotton top. The day looked inviting, so she locked the patio door and set off towards the beach, thinking she might meet Guy on the way. She followed the line of shrubs that led down towards the sea and acted as a natural boundary for the private beach.

Suddenly she heard someone shout, 'Hi!'

Peering through the bushes she saw a very tanned young man waving to her from the next patch. She stepped through a gap onto his side of the beach and he came sprinting up with a grin. Smiling blue eyes greeted her from beneath a well-groomed thatch of blond hair and she had an impression of a tightly honed body, all of which was set off by a perfect suntan.

'I'm Karl, your neighbour. Guess you're the new tenants, huh?'

'Only temporary,' she smiled, taking the hand that was held out to her. 'My name's Sara.'

'Had a look around yet?'

'Not really. We only arrived last night.'

'We?'

'I'm here with my husband, Guy.'

Was she mistaken, or did she detect a faintly disappointed expression on his handsome face? But surely he didn't imagine she could be staying at such a luxurious villa all by herself?

'What do you plan to do today?'

'I don't know. Guy's gone for a walk and I don't know when he'll be back.'

'In that case, why don't I show you around? We have some cute little boutiques and restaurants round here. You'll be one step up on your husband if you get to know about them before he does.'

The friendly invitation in his smile was irresistible. Sara nodded. 'OK.' She felt wicked as she followed him up the beach towards his equally luxurious-looking pad. This would serve Guy right for abandoning her like that.

Instead of walking, as she'd presumed they would, Karl led her into his garage and helped her into a beautiful white vintage sports car. She felt excited as he revved the engine, as much by the proximity of so much testosterone as by the prospect of the drive. Karl was the sort of character you saw in *Baywatch*, packed with solid muscle and with a face to make girls swoon. He was obviously very rich. Perhaps he was a Hollywood actor. Sara felt her insides bubbling with excitement as he manoeuvred the car out of the garage and onto the road, his hand brushing her knee as he changed gear with the old-fashioned lever.

Karl explained that they were heading for 'the village' along the Pacific Coast Highway and Sara stared, goggle-eyed, at everything they passed on the way. Suddenly she saw a familiar figure walking along the beach with his arm around two pretty girls. She wanted to cry out, 'Stop! There's my husband,' but the words choked in her throat and in a few seconds they had passed him by. She turned around, craning her neck to make sure it was him. Yes, it certainly was. And the two girls he'd picked up were busty blondes, flashing their assets in low-necked tops and mini-shorts.

Staring blankly at the road ahead, Sara felt her eyes fill with tears. Karl chatted on, oblivious, telling her about the J. Paul Getty museum, but she scarcely heard a word. Jealous anger was tormenting her, but at the same time she was exulting that she'd found a new companion too. If that was how Guy wanted to play it here in Malibu, then he wasn't the only one out to have some extramarital fun and games.

Chapter Four

NOT FOR THE first time in her married life, Sara had adultery in mind. As they drove through the chic neighbourhood in the classy little car, she could hardly keep her eyes, let alone her hands, off the handsome Karl. The casual ease with which he steered the sportster around, the well-defined muscles in his perfectly tanned arms and the exotic musk of his expensive aftershave, were all conspiring to turn her on a treat.

'Here we are – best place in town for a brunch!' he declared, pulling up outside a mewsy-looking cottage called Café au Coffee. A small cobbled courtyard was filling up with the Malibu smart set who all looked like famous film stars, although Sara was at a loss to put a specific name to any particular face. Karl got them a corner table and she studied the menu of a thousand choices.

'I think I'll just have a pastrami on rye with a coffee,' she said at last.

'Have you tried the hazelnut?'

'Hazelnut what?'

'Coffee. Or you could have almond, or pistachio.'

'Coffee that tastes of *nuts*?'

'Sure. They do a whole range of flavoured coffees here – see the back of the menu?'

'Can't I just have coffee-flavoured coffee?'

His white teeth were suddenly exposed in a huge grin. 'Yes, but why not live dangerously for once?'

The steel-blue eyes gleamed their subtext at her, clear as day. He was inviting her to take a chance on him, too. A wild pulse raced deep within her as she faced the temptation and wondered whether to give in to it. 'I'll try the hazelnut, thank you,' she told him, primly.

While he went to place their order inside the shop Sara recalled the sight of Guy strolling along with those two women, as if he had a perfect right to do so, and cold anger filled her veins once more. She had to hand it to him, he was a quick worker. He was acting as though winning the lottery had gone straight to his head like champagne, affecting his personality in weird ways.

That scene back at the villa had unnerved Sara, not least because she had half-enjoyed it. Guy had been brutal and selfish in his taking of her, but while the physical pain had shocked her, the feeling of being overpowered and completely at his mercy had aroused subtle feelings of satisfaction in her, as alien as they were potent. Now she had been, literally, taken for a ride by a complete stranger and she was experiencing something of the same excitement. What if he wanted to take her in that way too, to ravish her without compunction or even use her in ways that were unknown to her? How would she feel then?

Sensing that such speculation might prove dangerous, Sara quickly directed her mind to lighter things by the time Karl returned. 'This afternoon I thought I might do a little shopping,' she said. 'Can you tell me where the most fashionable shops are round here?'

'I could tell you, but I'd rather take you.' He smiled. 'This husband of yours – is he a possessive type, or would he let me have you for a few hours?'

Again ambiguity shone in his eyes as they raked over her, lingering perceptibly on the swell of her breasts as they peaked below her cotton top. Sara had not bothered to put on a bra and her nipples were jutting visibly, tingling with electricity in response to his gaze.

'Oh, I should think so,' she replied casually. 'But perhaps I'd better give him a ring.'

'There's a phone in there,' Karl said, pointing through the door of the shop.

Sara had a card with the phone number on. She sidled past the counter and tables inside the coffee shop and found the public phone. She found a quarter from the change Guy had given her and pushed it into the slot then dialled the number. It rang a few times, then the answerphone kicked in. 'Guy, since you didn't wait for me this morning, I went out by myself,' she began brusquely. 'It's now midday and I shall be going shopping this afternoon. See you back at the villa around five.'

Her conscience salved, she returned to the table where their food and drinks had arrived. She relaxed enough to laugh at Karl's rather feeble jokes and was soon enjoying herself. Relieved that he asked her no personal questions, she was content to talk about England in general and London in particular, about her favourite films and actors, and the things she would like to see in Los Angeles.

Afterwards Karl escorted her like a perfect gentleman to several small boutiques, where Sara had fun trying on the most outrageous clothes, things she would never dream of wearing. She enjoyed parading before him in the garments since he showed genuine interest, unlike Guy who always hated it when she went shopping for clothes. Karl's blue eyes lit up with enthusiasm whenever she emerged from the changing rooms, and his solemn appraisal of each garment made her giggle.

The gold lamé jump suit was received with a considered, 'Well, it's OK, so long as you wear shades. Otherwise, if you caught sight of yourself in a mirror you might go blind!' When she put on a gown that was little more than a few scraps of black chiffon strategically held together by thin straps, he commented, 'No matter what function you attend in that little number you'll never feel overdressed.' And his response to a slinky purple satin swimsuit with a plunge neckline was, 'Sinful, baby, just sinful!'

Corny as his humour was, it brightened Sara's day and she realised that ever since the lottery win she had been waiting to have just this kind of fun. She wanted to be with people who took life lightly, who used their wealth to bring themselves and other people happiness, but all she seemed to have had since the fateful win was trouble, from one quarter or another. She didn't want to go back to the villa and have to face Guy's lies or, worse, his boasting about his new conquests. She wanted to have a good time herself, and Karl had 'good-time guy' written all over his young, handsome, self-assured face.

Sara bought herself half a new wardrobe of clothes that were frivolous without being outrageous: beachwear, a glitzy evening dress, wonderfully tailored shorts and trousers, a superbly flattering little top. And shoes. A pair of gorgeous strappy sandals, red high heels and a stylish, comfy pair that fitted her like a glove. She bought accessories too: designer shades, a tooled Italian leather belt and bag, a couple of kooky hats. Jewellery she was more cautious about. She didn't want to buy rocks or vulgar, flashy stuff. In the end she bought just a discreet gold chain, a gold bracelet studded with tiny diamonds and a sapphire and pearl ring that she simply fell in love with.

Every time she used her gold credit card Karl's eyes seemed to flash wider. Not that he appeared to lack funds himself, of course, but she could tell he was impressed by this English woman throwing her money around like there was no tomorrow. Sara thought she might invent a new identity for herself – a title perhaps, a wealthy family or a successful business. Her story must be that her fortune had been obtained in her own right, and in some perfectly reputable manner. She certainly didn't want it to be by gambling.

For the time being, however, Sara volunteered no information about her background and Karl had the good manners not to inquire. She enjoyed behaving as if she were used to spending this kind of money every day. Fortunately she was spreading her purchases amongst several shops; otherwise they might have become suspicious and subjected her to an embarrassing credit check.

Sara found that being so extravagant was a real turn-on. It gave her such a sense of power and wellbeing, filled her with such a wonderfully heady elation that she was drunk with it all, drunk and randy, even though she'd had nothing more stimulating than a couple of coffees. Of course, the presence of a gorgeous hunk at her side did help a little, and the prospect that they might retreat to his beach house later and make love, just a stone's throw from where Guy might be waiting anxiously for her to return, was adding spice to her appetite too.

'All done?' he enquired at last, one dark-blond eyebrow quizzically raised.

'Yes. What a wonderful spending spree! Heaven knows how I'm going to transport it all to the UK – I'll have to chuck out all my old clothes.'

The prospect delighted her. An entirely new image, that's what she needed. For a few seconds her imagination took wing as she pictured the new, improved Sara Kingsley. Then she turned to her escort with a grin. 'But I suppose I'd better get all this stuff back to the villa now.'

Karl had other ideas. 'Wouldn't you like to go for a spin first? There's a wonderful little beach I know, not far from here. It's private, but I'm a friend of the owner and she lets me use it whenever I like.'

His blue eyes held a hint of mystery and Sara was intrigued. She was also finding him very desirable. Parading before him in all those reveal-ing clothes had heightened the sexual charge between them, making it even more obvious that the attraction was mutual. She nodded and Karl led her back to the car with half a dozen presti-giously tagged bags hanging from each of their arms.

It was wonderful to drive along the beautiful coastline in the early afternoon sun. On one side were rocky slopes covered with flowering shrubs and topped with coastal redwoods, while on the other side were rock-strewn Pacific beaches and the cold blue of the ocean. Sara felt as if she were in some Hollywood film as the open-top car wound its serpentine way along the highway with a light breeze ruffling her hair.

When Karl turned into the grounds of a vast, hacienda-style villa she gasped at the opulence of the place. Perfect lawns and carefully tended flower beds led down through terraces towards the beach. As she followed him along a winding paved path Sara couldn't resist asking, 'Who lives here – some film star?'

He turned with a grin and held out his hand. 'She's been in films, yes, but you won't have heard of her. I can't tell you her name because she guards her privacy, but I can assure you there's no prob-lem about us using her beach. Come on, we have to go through here.'

Once they were walking on the silvery sand Sara realised that the beach was even more private than the one at the Villa Mariposa. Rocky headlands covered in thick vegetation curved out on either side, making the beach completely invisible except from the ocean. And since, as Karl explained, there were treacherous rocks out there, not many vessels dared to come in close enough to view the beach.

'My friend often holds parties here,' Karl told her, moving towards the sun loungers that were already in place, each one bearing a neatly folded towel and bottle of suntan lotion. 'And we always swim in the nude.'

The thought sent a quiver of excitement running through Sara's veins. She watched him start to strip off and knew that he expected her to follow suit. Well, why not? It would be good to get an all-over tan. Slowly she undid her sandals, feasting her eyes on Karl's delightful body all the while. She quickly took in his lean, sturdy thighs and his strong back and shoulders, but her gaze lingered with greatest appreciation on the twin hemispheres of his buttocks. They were just as biscuit-coloured as the rest of him and the flesh was perfectly round and smooth, inviting her touch. He turned round and she only just managed to stifle a gasp as she saw his cock raised to half-mast.

It was a fair-sized organ and very attractive, with its honey-coloured shaft and pink circumcised glans. Mentally she compared it unfavourably with Guy's pallid equipment and then felt guilty. It wasn't fair to criticise a man for what he was born with. Yet her pussy had no such scruples. It yearned unashamedly to embrace that fine prick, to taste its sweet essence.

Karl saw where her gaze was directed and gave a grin. 'Will you cream me?' he asked, picking up a tube of Ambre Solaire and holding it out to her. He leapt onto the sun-bed and lay there on his side, regarding her closely. His prick had swollen considerably and was sticking up at a perky angle, making it difficult for Sara to take her eyes off it. She froze where she stood, barefoot in the sand, wondering exactly what he wanted her to do for him.

'I love being creamed by a woman's soft touch.'

Sara felt her whole body tingle with a mixture of lust and fear. Although the man seemed harmless enough, she had no idea what she was getting herself into. What if he was some kind of sadist? He could perform unspeakable acts on her in this secluded spot, kill her even and dispose of her body by simply throwing it into the ocean. Who would know? She cursed herself for not at least mentioning who she was with on her answer-phone message. After all, this was America, where violence was a daily occurrence.

'It's all right, you know.' Karl's voice shook her out of her state of terrified suspense. 'I won't make you do anything you don't want to.'

It was the cue she had been waiting for. Relieved, Sara pulled her top over her head and felt the warm air caress her naked breasts. She took the tube of cream and squeezed a blob onto her palm. 'Back or front?' she asked in a businesslike tone.

In response Karl turned over lazily on the sun-bed, rearranging his bulky genitalia before he settled completely. Sara took off her shorts and knelt down in her white lace panties, somehow reluctant to bare herself completely. She could feel the hot sun on her back and knew that, once she was finished with Karl, she would demand the same service from him. The thought of his strong, brown hands rubbing her breasts made her nipples throb and her vagina contract with sudden hunger.

His skin felt wonderfully warm and smooth as she began to stroke over the muscled expanse of his back. Sara's fingertips skimmed down his spine, probing each of the vertebrae beneath their

fleshy padding, and she heard Karl groan his satisfied response. She spread her palms over his shoulders and rubbed in the protective cream. It was like
caressing a big cat. She could feel the dormant
power of his muscles and her pussy was responding juicily, soaking through her panties onto her
thighs.

Down his lean back she swept until her hands
rested on the firm mounds of his bottom. Karl
groaned again as she began to rub the tightly
contoured buttocks. Compared to Guy's flabby
backside, it was a model of sculptured perfection.
She let just one finger trail down the ravine
between them and the little hairs prickled against
her skin, making her even more excited. He shifted
voluptuously, parting his thighs a little more to
enable her to view his heavy testicles in their dark
amber sac.

Sara was tempted to fondle them but thought
better of it. It seemed too much of a liberty. She was
still unsure whether this encounter would turn
sexual. What if he only wanted her to protect him
from the sun then lie quietly beside him while they
both toasted? It seemed unlikely, but she wasn't
going to make the first move. She smoothed her
way down his rigid thighs and calves, pausing at
his feet.

Slowly Karl turned over, his cock springing up
so suddenly that she had to smother a giggle. He
seemed unconcerned by the fact that he had a real
hard on now. Sara could feel her pulse thudding in
her ears as she began to spread the cream up his
shins and over his knees, wondering what on earth
she would do when she had to anoint his stomach.
Should she hold his erection out of the way with

one hand while she rubbed in the cream with the other? The thought of touching that rampant organ was bringing her out in a bad case of prickly heat. It looked so primed that it might go off in her hand, like a stick of dynamite.

'You don't have to handle my cock if you don't want to,' Karl told her, displaying an uncanny ability to read her mind. His eyes met hers with calm assurance. Demonstrating his telepathic skill even more he added, 'But you do want to touch it, don't you? I can tell.'

Sara lowered her eyes with an embarrassed shrug. She had reached his thighs now and was spreading the scented cream slowly over them, inching towards his groin. The action was mesmeric, lulling her into a strange state. She could feel the heat of the sun on her back and the trickle of sweat that was running between her swaying breasts as she worked, squatting on her heels, one of which was tucked enticingly near her crotch.

'Do whatever you want with me,' Karl continued, placing his hands behind his head and gazing skyward. He gave a long, contented sigh before adding, 'I'm yours, completely.'

Sara finally plucked up the courage to look the quivering member in the eye. It was near to bursting with robust desire, the pink tip stretched and shiny while the shaft was like smooth plastic. A pearly bead was oozing from the slit and Sara had a sudden urge to wipe it clean with her tongue. She bent her head and, taking the root of the shaft firmly between her finger and thumb, licked across the tumid glans until it was covered with a thin film of her saliva and a taste of musk lingered on her tongue.

'More,' Karl murmured sleepily.

Fully engorged, his cock presented quite a challenge. It reared impatiently in her tentative grasp and Sara began to give it the stimulation it craved, sliding her semi-closed hand up and down the velvet-smooth shank. When she came to the top her thumb rubbed gently at the viscous ball, making it spill more of its precious juice. Soon her mouth was watering. It was a long time since she'd given anyone an enthusiastic blow job – too long. Used to Guy's not very aesthetically pleasing penis she had forgotten how attractive a man's equipment could be, and this one was a superb example.

Warming to the task and feeling wanton, Sara took off her panties and straddled Karl's outstretched legs. She moved up his thighs, their hairiness mildly abrasive against the sensitive tissues of her labia. With one hand she gathered up the loose scrotum and held it to her wet and tingling vulva, then she bent her head once again to take the tip of his prick between her lips. He groaned as she took the whole of his glans into her mouth and then massaged her vulva with his scrotum.

With her thumb hooked firmly into the hot little niche that held her clitoris, Sara proceeded to stimulate herself while she fellated him. She could feel herself throbbing urgently now, and Karl must have been aware of her need for stimulation because he reached out and touched her nipples. He was not near enough to caress her breasts, but he could pull at her tumid nipples with his fingertips, providing her with the most exquisitely tantalising sensations as his erection pushed hard against the roof of her mouth, seeking its own satisfaction.

The heat was burning its way down Sara's spine as she became totally absorbed in their mutual pleasuring, and she was scarcely aware whether it was coming from the sun or from her own sexuality. She realigned Karl's demanding organ so that it was angled towards her throat and soon her mouth was filled with hot, pulsating flesh, so filling that her tongue could scarcely find its way around it. Sucking strongly, she felt the throb between her labia turn into a raging hunger and knew that she would soon be satisfied.

When her climax came it was darkly sensual, full of the thrill of the forbidden. Her quivering thighs seemed to excite Karl too and his orgasmic juices streamed down her throat as he groaned aloud. Dazed and utterly spent, Sara collapsed sideways onto the hot sand and lay oblivious for a few seconds before she came to and sought some refuge from the punishing sun. 'I must have shade!' she gasped, but instead of fiddling with the umbrella over her sun-bed she made for the cool green of the trees that skirted the beach.

Karl remained where he was, languid and relaxed, his body glistening with oil and sweat. What have I done? Sara wondered, coming to her senses again. For a few seconds guilt assailed her, but then she remembered Guy and his two pretty escorts and her feelings of shame turned to anger. Was he enjoying himself in a threesome at that very moment? Suddenly she wanted to make him jealous, to inflict upon him what she herself had felt.

Tucked away in her cool haven, she was

surprised to see a woman suddenly arrive on the scene and make straight for Karl's sun-bed. She wore a pleated white dress with a halter neck that was an almost exact replica of the infamous Marilyn Monroe one. Sara was thinking about getting up and making herself known to her when the woman casually stripped off her dress and revealed that she was wearing no underwear. Then she slipped out of her gold sandals and began to caress Karl's tousled head. Was this the owner of the magnificent villa on the hillside? Curiosity kept Sara rooted to the spot as she stared into the middle distance, scrutinising the woman's face and figure.

It was obvious that she was forty-something, but extremely well preserved. Her golden tan enhanced her firm, jutting breasts and equally toned behind, while her blonde hair was coiled into loose ringlets. Sara couldn't get a good view of her face, but she had an impression of pouting pink lips and large, lustrous eyes. Definitely film-star material. Karl was looking up at her now, a huge grin on his face, and Sara could hear their murmured greetings.

Evidently he was no longer interested in anyone else, because his absorption in the proceedings was total. Sara gasped as the woman began fondling his resting dick, which revived in seconds into a rampant erection. The woman wasted no time. As soon as his erection was restored she lowered herself onto it and began to ride lazily up and down, her ample breasts swaying rhythmically. The casual way in which the encounter proceeded staggered Sara, but her embarrassment kept her in the background, a mesmerised voyeur.

The sight of such unabashed sexuality was turning her on, reviving the hot flood of her libido once more. Unable to help herself, Sara began to fondle her breasts, feeling the nipples harden beneath her deft fingers. She pinched them to stiff peaks, squeezed the fullness of her breasts and felt the electric current of her arousal wing its way to her clitoris where it throbbed and buzzed. With one finger she explored her vulva, feeling herself still lubricated, and found the spot where she most liked to be stimulated. Rubbing gently at first, she luxuriated in the pleasurable sensations while she watched the distant couple similarly engaged.

Suddenly she saw the woman climb off her lover, throw a towel onto the hot sand and kneel down on all fours. The sight of Karl's huge cock made Sara gasp with renewed longing, but in a matter of seconds he was taking the woman from behind, thrusting hard against the twin cushions of her buttocks with a series of grunts and groans. The energetic display was too much for Sara, who began to masturbate frantically, unable to hold off the impending climax any longer.

Her second orgasm was even more violent than the first, sending her into a series of shuddering spasms that flushed through her body like wildfire. When she opened her eyes again she could see the woman collapsed on the towel with Karl on top of her and guessed that the pair had reached their climax, too. She sat back against the trunk of a palm, closed her eyes and wondered what the hell to do now.

The next time Sara opened her eyes it was to see the woman walking back up the beach with her white dress slung casually over her shoulder. Karl lay supine, his eyes now protected by a pair of expensive shades and a towel lying across his midriff. The woman began to climb slowly up the steps that led to the elegant gardens and the white villa beyond, her attractive rear swaying on the high gold heels as she ascended. Their encounter had only lasted ten very intense minutes and Sara was intrigued. Evidently they were old friends.

Pretending she had just awoken from a long doze, Sara walked slowly across the shore towards the spot where Karl lay. He heard her coming and lowered the glasses onto his nose, surveying her quizzically. His mouth twisted into a wry grin, he said, 'I forgot you were still here, my little English rose. Ready to go back yet?'

Sara realised he wanted to pretend nothing had happened. She decided to play the same game. His behaviour had been so bizarre that she didn't want to antagonise him in case he was totally out to lunch. 'Mm, I suppose so. If you wouldn't mind.'

He sat up, retrieving his discarded clothes. 'No problem. I have to get back myself.'

There was no sign of the mysterious woman when they walked through the grounds or past the house, although Sara couldn't help wondering whether they were being observed from one of the windows. Karl never mentioned her on the way back and Sara was disinclined to raise the subject, but as they were walking from the car towards their respective beach homes he said, 'Maybe you'd like to come out to the villa again sometime?'

The thought was both exciting and terrifying. There had been an air of decadence about the place, borne out by the casual way in which the strange woman had taken her pleasure, as if she were used to making use of her guests in that way. Sara muttered something non-committal and, after thanking Karl sincerely for taking her shopping, grabbed her bags and scurried off towards the gate of the Villa Mariposa.

'Who the hell was that?'

Guy's angry outburst as she walked through the door made Sara see red. She was about to tell him that she knew all about his dalliance with the two nymphets, but then changed her mind. Perhaps it was best if she played the innocent for a while.

'Our neighbour, a nice guy called Karl. He offered to take me shopping in his sports car. Look what I bought!'

She threw the bags down on the sofa with a smile. Guy looked wary, but said nothing as she proceeded to pull her frocks and shoes and jewels out of their stylish carrier bags. He followed her through to the kitchen when she went to mix herself some fresh juice from the selection of fruits in the fridge, and she asked him where he'd been all day.

'Oh, out and about,' he answered vaguely. 'I meant to get back for breakfast but it was so nice, I walked further than I meant to, and by the time I got back you'd gone.'

'I see.'

The lie hurt, but Sara was determined to brave it out. She changed the subject by asking what he wanted to do for supper, and they agreed to order Chinese from the delicious-looking menu they found at the villa. While they waited on the terrace with drinks in their hands Sara felt her seething anger fade into indifference. What if Guy had been flirting with other women? What if she had played around with their handsome neighbour? They were millionaires, and everything was different now.

Guy expressed similar sentiments as they ate their *dim sum* on the patio with the sun sinking slowly into the ocean before them. 'I'm just beginning to realise what having money means.' His dark eyes were gazing at the horizon, filled with brooding. 'What's the point of having loads if you can't do as you like? And I don't just mean spending it, either.'

'Then what do you mean, Guy?' Sara heard her voice tremble with apprehension.

'I'm talking about having a good time. A really good time, no holds barred. I'm fed up with being respectable, keeping my nose clean. I want to break a few rules, kick over the traces. After all, we're only young once. When I look back on how we've been for the past couple of years, I realise what a straitjacket I was in.'

Sara stared at him in dismay. 'Come to the point, Guy,' she snapped.

'OK.' When he turned to face her his expression was unreadable and a sick dread seized her. Was this to be the end of their marriage, here on a deserted Californian shore so far from everything, and everyone, she'd ever known? But then his face broke into a grin. 'Don't look so scared, love. I'm just talking about us both having more freedom to do as we fancy.'

'To do *who* we fancy – isn't that what you mean?'

He looked sheepish. 'I suppose so. But can you blame me? Here we are on the edge of Hollywood, surrounded by some of the most beautiful people on the planet. Wouldn't it be crazy to take a "look but don't touch" attitude?'

'Maybe. I can't deny it would be exciting. But won't it be the beginning of the end for you and me? I'm scared, Guy.'

His expression was sad as he took her hand. 'I think it's already too late for us, isn't it? We've been sliding downhill fast for ages. Admit it. This lottery business has just put things into perspective, hasn't it?'

Sara couldn't find it in her heart to deny what he said. In one way she was relieved. Like him, she had wanted to have more sexual freedom, but she had been too timid to take it until that afternoon, when her self-control had finally snapped in the face of overwhelming temptation. In a flash of insight she realised that she had struggled to keep their marriage going out of duty, not love. 'What will become of us?' she asked, wanly.

Guy put his arm around her shoulders and pulled her closer to him. He planted a soft kiss on her forehead. 'You'll always be special to me, kitten.'

Hot tears stung her eyes as she nestled against him in the fading light. It was true, there was no chemistry between them any more, only friendship. Yet when she thought about the future a cold dread seized her. Was she just clinging to the past out of feebleness?

'I was stupid to be jealous when I saw you with that guy from next door,' Guy went on. 'If you want to have a fling with him, go ahead. You're free. I give you just the same liberty as I give myself.'

There was little joy in her heart as she asked, 'So what happens now? I saw you with those two girls this morning. Do you want to spend the rest of the time with them?'

'Maybe. But one thing we have to do is stop interrogating each other. We must let go, Sara. It won't be easy at first, but there's no option if we both want to be free. And it's definitely what I want. How about you?'

Sara looked straight into his brown eyes, searching for some hint of the old Guy, the man she had loved and married, but he wasn't there. Instead she saw a man determined to make up for lost time, determined to enjoy himself at all costs, and she knew it wasn't worth opposing him. Her only option was to accept the situation and find what happiness she could for herself.

'All right, if that's truly what you want, then I'm in agreement.'

He kissed her again, gently on the lips, and tears prickled behind her closed lids once again. She rose from the table, needing to be alone. Indoors she put some music on and lay down on the huge sofa with her feet up, trying not to think. The moment she had been trying to stave off for months was finally upon her and she felt nothing but emptiness.

Minutes later Sara heard female voices calling from the far end of the beach. 'Guy? Are you there, Guy?' She knew instinctively that it was the same two girls she'd seen him with that morning. He didn't call back but she knew he had gone to them, following his dick as he longed to do, as he'd said he would.

And she couldn't find it in her heart to blame him.

Chapter Five

WHEN GUY DIDN'T return that night Sara was forced to review her options. She could either cause a scene and make things worse for both of them, or admit defeat and go her own way. Whether that would include behaving the same way as Guy, latching onto any fanciable partner who came her way, was still in doubt. To indulge in the kind of promiscuity she had only ever dreamed about was risky, especially in a foreign country. Yet she longed for some release from her importunate desires.

After a restless night she rose early and, finding herself still alone in the villa, wandered out onto the beach. The sky was pastel-pale and seemed limitless, making Sara think about her own expanded horizons. At first her thoughts were bitter. What use were millions if her marriage was going down the pan? Yet in her heart she knew that winning the lottery had only speeded up an inevitable process. Perhaps she should be grateful that there would be no financial problems following their divorce, and it could all be accomplished amicably.

Divorce? Sara frowned as she paddled at the water's edge, her cotton skirt drifting about her calves. Guy had made no mention of it. Perhaps he envisaged them carrying on in some kind of open marriage. Or maybe he only wanted his freedom on holiday. Sara realised that she had no real idea of what he had in mind, and they needed to have a serious talk sometime. But for now she was free, free as air.

How long had it been since she felt like this? Her mind zipped back to her teenage years, when boyfriends had come and gone on an almost weekly basis as she tried out first a dark-haired scholar, then a blond sportsman, then a sensitive artistic type followed by a crazy scientist. It had been fun, all that experimenting . . .

'Good morning.'

No sooner had she recognised Karl than a huge wet dog came bounding up and shook droplets all over her. She stroked his dark, wet mane, laughing as Karl approached with long strides. 'And how are you this morning?' he asked.

Sara smiled, noting his crisp blue and white T-shirt, expensive trainers and navy shorts. He'd evidently been exercising along with his dog, his forehead showing a light film of sweat. 'I'm very well, thank you,' she replied, feeling awkward when she remembered what had happened the previous day. What temporary madness had come over her? Yet he showed no sign of treating her with anything but the utmost respect.

'I'm glad I caught you, as a matter of fact. I wanted to invite you and your husband over for a meal tonight. I've a couple of other guests I'd like you to meet.'

'Oh . . . er . . . I'm not sure what Guy's doing,' she hedged.

'It will be quite casual, no need to dress up. Perhaps you could ask him and let me know before . . . say, five this afternoon?'

She nodded, swallowing her embarrassment. To admit that she had no idea when she would next see her husband would be so humiliating. But she didn't know how long she could keep up the pretence with their neighbour.

Sara spent the day by the pool, sunning herself, swimming and reading. It was relaxing, and yet she couldn't help wondering what she would say to Karl when he phoned her at five. There had been no word from Guy and she had a feeling that he might be away for several days. It was just the sort of thing he would do, to prove that he meant what he said about them going their separate ways.

When Karl phoned she said her husband had gone out and she didn't know when he'd be back. It seemed better not to be too specific. 'What a shame,' Karl said. 'I was looking forward to meeting him. But you're very welcome to come by yourself, Sara. My friend Romero is a wonderful cook. You'd love his food.'

It was tempting. Sara was tired of her own company and had no wish to be there in the villa if Guy did choose to come home, waiting for him like a dutiful wife. She accepted readily, but then Karl said, 'Unfortunately one of my other guests had to drop out too, so there'll be just the three of us. Never mind, you know what they say: "Three's a crowd." See you around eight, darling!'

This was a chance to dress up in one of her new outfits. Sara took full advantage of the time available to her. First she got into the spa bath, wallowing in *Giorgio Aire* that filled her head with exotic fruit, linden blossom and a hint of Californian poppy. She washed her hair and towelled it into a fluffy cloud, letting it dry naturally. The expensive cut she'd had in London before she came away was serving her beautifully. Then she smoothed after-sun lotion into her body with voluptuous relish before putting on pristine white lace underwear and sitting before the well-lit mirror to do her make-up.

It was ages since she'd been this excited about a date, Sara reflected, as she made siren eyes the way the salon make-up artist had shown her. They shone back at her in the mirror, a seductive shade of jade, thanks to clever highlighting. After outlining her mouth in burnt orange she filled it in with a peachy shade, making her lips appear full and shapely. The light tan she had already acquired enhanced the healthy glow in her cheeks, making her look years younger. Or was it winning all that money which made the difference?

Peering closely at herself Sara was convinced that many of the wrinkles she'd had around the eyes were starting to fade. Perhaps worrying about money had made her old before her time. Or was it the prospect of a new lover that was so rejuvenating? Her glance dropped to the way her new bra pushed up her breasts into seductive mounds with a deep ravine between them. Suddenly she felt a keen pang of desire shoot through her as she saw herself through Karl's eyes. How wonderful to be desired by a hunk like him!

Even so, she was very nervous by the time she walked round to his door. The slinky green and white dress showed every curve and hollow of her body, it was so soft and clinging, while her white strappy sandals accentuated her long, honey-gold legs. She knew she looked alluring, but had she overdone it? For a second or two, as she approached his door, she had cold feet and considered chickening out, but she forced herself to go ahead and once she'd rung his bell there was no backing off.

The way his eyes lit up the instant he saw her convinced Sara that it had all been worth it.

'You look like a million dollars!' He grinned.

'Funny you should say that,' Sara couldn't help responding. But he wouldn't let it go and asked what she meant. In the end she decided to come clean. 'I won the National Lottery,' she admitted impulsively. 'Me and Guy between us, that is. I still can't get over it.'

'This calls for champagne!' Karl said, leading her through into his spacious sitting room where a very good-looking young man was seated on a leather sofa. 'Sara, meet Romero. He's an old friend of mine.'

Romero rose at once and offered her his hand. He was a sexy Latin type, with a touch of Sly Stallone about him, and Sara was instantly smitten. The way his velvet-brown eyes caressed her whole body from a distance was evidence that he was equally attracted to her. Sara took his warm, lean hand in hers for a second or two longer than was proper at first meeting. She felt her pulse beat a wild tattoo as she sank into the embrace of a soft leather armchair next to the sofa.

'So, Sara, you have sudden riches? That must be very nice!'

Romero's deep, mellow voice bore just a trace of a foreign accent. It was easy to imagine him murmuring naughty things into her ear and Sara felt a thrill of anticipation pass through her. What did Karl have planned for the evening? Remembering what she had experienced and witnessed on that remote beach the previous day, she had a feeling that he might be intending to serve her up as an extra course at the end of the meal. So long as the dishy Romero was included, she would have no objections.

'It's a bit strange, all this,' she said, as a thin flute of pale yellow bubbles was placed in her hand. 'I'm not quite used to it yet. I doubt if I'll ever be.'

'As long as you enjoy it.' Karl smiled. 'Here's to whatever pleasure money can buy.'

'I'll drink to that.' Romero grinned.

Sara watched the champagne enter his wide, sensual mouth. The tip of his pink tongue licked his lips afterwards with gutsy appreciation and Sara felt her innards take a dive. She gave a soft groan that became a gurgle as the fizzy drink hit her palate, its acidity prickling her taste buds. She swallowed her mouthful and made light of it. 'I could get used to this,' she quipped.

'Time to check on the first course,' Romero said, moving towards the wonderful aroma issuing from the kitchen.

'He's a marvellous cook,' Karl said, as soon as they were alone. 'Used to work in a famous Hollywood restaurant. He knows all the stars personally. You should see his flat. It's stuffed from floor to ceiling with signed photos.'

'Has he ever been in a film himself?' Sara asked, convinced that with looks like that he must have been snapped up at some time.

Karl gave a knowing laugh. He called through

to the kitchen, 'Hey, Romero! Sara wants to know if you've ever been in the movies.'

Romero reappeared with a sizzling pan in his hand. He was grinning broadly. 'Want to show her some of my videos?'

'I'm not sure we know her well enough for that.'

It dawned on Sara just what kind of 'videos' they might be referring to, and she felt herself blush. Was Romero, in addition to his other talents, some kind of porn actor? This was L.A., where everyone wanted to be a star. Recalling what she'd heard about the main qualification for being a male lead in those films, she found herself becoming even more intrigued.

No more was said, but there was a tension in the air that Sara found both intriguing and disquieting. She and Karl sat at a round table, exquisitely laid with fine china, silver and glass with a porcelain vase of perfect rosebuds in the centre, while Romero served two perfect works of art. Nestling on a bed of fresh leaves was a ball of prawn and avocado mousse of mouthwatering delicacy, garnished with just the right amount of orange zest and accompanied by soft, yeasty rolls straight from the oven.

'Oh, this is *so* delicious!' Sara exclaimed as the subtle bouquet of flavours hit her tongue.

'You ain't seen nothin' yet, lady,' Karl said. 'Wait till you taste his rack of baby lamb with glazed turnips and mangetout.'

Romero's particular combination of fabulous face and body, sexy voice and brilliant culinary skills was almost too much for Sara. She began to wonder about his bedroom prowess too. The man seemed very keen to please her, questioning her minutely about every aspect of his cooking, refilling her glass whenever it was half empty and showing an apparently genuine interest in everything she said. Would he be as attentive in bed? she found herself wondering.

'And your husband . . . Is he enjoying his holiday?'

Karl's question had an edge to it that brought Sara up short. She floundered, and the two men noticed. Karl continued, 'Tell me to mind my own business, by all means, but it seems to me you're spending an awful lot of time on your own, darling. If I was your husband I think I'd want to keep you by my side all the while, especially when you're so far from home.'

Sara swallowed frantically as her eyes started to brim and her throat began constricting in panic. Romero reached across the table and took her hand. His grip was firm and sure, giving her the strength to say, 'You're right. Things aren't going well between us. It's been coming for a long time and I suppose winning the lottery was the last straw.' She gave a bitter laugh. 'Everyone thinks you must be happy as Larry because you have all that money. But, like they say, it can't buy you love.'

'Poor Sara.' Romero got up and came round to her side of the table. He squatted down beside her chair looking up at her with his soulful brown eyes like a soppy dog. 'Tell you what, honey, why don't you put your feet up on that sofa while I make you one of my special coffees? It's even better than my raspberry dessert.'

Sara smiled, feeling relieved that she didn't have to pretend any more. Karl led her to the sofa and tenderly removed her sandals, then began to massage her bare feet. It was incredibly soothing, but soon she felt aroused too as the rhythmic strokes of his fingers moved up her calves and shins. She was very conscious of the fact that, beneath her dress and half-slip, she was wearing only panties and a bra.

Karl's fingers moved lazily around her knees and she thought of their encounter on the beach the day before. Boldly she asked, 'Did you see your friend yesterday, the one whose house we visited?'

He laughed. 'Oh, I saw her, all right. But only briefly.'

Sara had a sudden vision of the woman riding astride him, her blonde hair flowing free and her shapely breasts bobbing with the rhythmic exertion. She could scarcely suppress a smile.

Romero returned with a fragrant coffee. She took a sip and tasted almond liqueur along with the finest Jamaican Blue Mountain beans. A purist might have objected to the adulteration of the coffee but to Sara it was bliss. She took several sips then lay back and closed her eyes, waiting for the caffeine hit. She could feel her head start to clear. The constant muddle she'd been in since Guy had gone off with his new girlfriends had begun to sort itself out, ridding her of the guilt she felt.

Being in the company of two sexy males was boosting her confidence tremendously, and when she felt those caressing hands move higher than her knees a shiver of desire plunged her into hot anticipation, putting paid to any lingering doubts. She could feel Romero's gentle hands on her forehead, soothing away any tension, and she sighed as her body subsided into a voluptuous calm. With

Karl at her feet and Romero at her head she was about to get a top-to-toe massage, and the prospect made her purr with pleasure.

Karl gently pushed up the hem of her expensive silk dress and began to stroke her inner thighs. His touch was incredibly light, almost tickling, but very erotic. In the secret niche of her sex Sara felt her clitoris bloom and grow, becoming sensitised. At the same time Romero was brushing her neck with light, exciting kisses while his fingers crept around the neck of her dress making her faint with longing. Both men were expert teasers and soon she was craving more of their attention, wanting to feel their hands and lips in more intimate places.

'Such lovely skin,' she heard Romero murmur as his mouth left her neck to travel along her collar-bone. Beneath the silkiness of her dress Sara's breasts were swelling with arousal in their tight, uplifting bra and she longed to be free from all constriction. Her tantalising lovers were in no hurry, however, and she was too timid to rush them. Although her body was keyed up like a finely tuned instrument, with every nerve stretched almost to breaking point, she knew she would have to be patient.

'Poor little rich girl,' Romero whispered, returning to bite softly at her ear lobe. 'Don't worry, Karl and I will make you feel better. We know how to make a pretty woman feel special, don't we, Karl?'

'We certainly do.' Karl chuckled. He was raising the hem of her dress now, exposing all of her restless thighs to his caresses. Sara wriggled in delight as his hands smoothed their way up and down, his fingertips just brushing the damp lacy pouch that concealed her sex.

Romero's fingers were becoming more adventurous too. They crept beneath the neckline of her dress and found the swell of her breasts, passing from one to the other before plunging momentarily into the cleavage between them. His lips made their way to her mouth and soon they were kissing deeply, with Sara relishing the sweetness of his tongue as it met hers in friendly combat.

He was a good kisser, active without being overpowering, and soon it was Sara who was urging him on with eager lips and running fevered fingers through his sleek locks. His hair felt incredibly thick and luxuriant, and soon she felt him repaying the compliment, his fingers plunging recklessly into her own golden tresses and making her scalp tingle.

Sara's attention was divided as she became aware of Karl's steady progress up her thighs towards the increasingly damp mound of her delta. The skirt of her dress was pushed right up and she could feel his hot breath fan her vulva through the thin lace of her panties. Slowly he pressed his mouth right into her labia in a lingering kiss through the thin material that had her squirming with frustration. But then he went on to the bare skin of her stomach, titillating her with whisper-soft touches of his lips that only increased her arousal.

Meanwhile Romero was travelling down her cleavage with his mouth, making little lizard-like darts of his tongue to tease the sensitive tops of her breasts. Sara gave a low moan, finding the dual assault upon her senses almost unendurable. The two men were practically meeting in the middle, but her clothes were starting to feel like an intolerable encumbrance and she longed to be free of them. Unable to help herself, she began to tear down the straps of her dress and wriggle free. It had cost a fortune, but if either man had taken a knife and ripped it off her she wouldn't have cared right then.

They were both far too gentlemanly to do that, of course. Romero found the zipper at the back and began to pull it down, letting her shoulders shrug off the straps and expose the cups of her strapless bra. Sara had a glimpse of his eyes as he caught sight of her swelling breasts and they were gleaming with lust. Then Karl took hold of the dress from below and pulled it down over her hips until she was wearing only her scanty underwear. Locked in a voluptuous dream, Sara could only lie in helpless abandon as the tide of desire swept over her.

Dimly she was aware that her two lovers had changed places; that now Romero was kneeling beside her thighs while Karl had come to kiss the entrapped globes of her breasts. Soon deft fingers were rolling down her panties and brushing against the soft curls of her pubic hair, making her shudder. She opened her thighs and raised her hips to enable the garment to be removed. At the same time Karl was pulling down the lacy cups of her bra to expose her erect nipples, and when she felt him take one between his moist lips she almost swooned with the extremity of her passion.

For a long time Sara kept her eyes closed in bliss, scarcely aware of who was making love to her, hardly conscious of what was being done even. All she knew was that this was the most fantastic sexual experience she had ever had. The level of sensuality was beyond her wildest dreams. She knew that her body was poised on the brink of orgasm and would remain so until she was penetrated, but when would that be? Neither of her lovers seemed to be in any hurry. Now Karl was nibbling softly at one breast while he caressed the other, tweaking her nipples into solid pink cones, while Romero seemed content to kiss all round her outer labia without venturing further inside.

'Sara,' she heard Karl murmur, smelling the rich combination of spicy aftershave and musk that was emanating from his pores. It was driving her wild. She reached up and pulled his mouth to hers, relishing the way he thrust straight in with his tongue. Would his cock behave in the same self-confident manner? she wondered, feeling her womb give a little jump of joy at the thought.

But it was not Karl's member that was destined to pleasure her, as she soon found out. Opening her eyes a little, just to regale herself with the sight of handsome Romero – or should that be 'Romeo'? – making love to her, Sara saw that he had somehow contrived to strip himself and was kneeling at her side stark-naked.

Unable to take her eyes off his muscled body, Sara examined the dark bronze torso with its strongly delineated curves and planes, then her gaze dropped unerringly to his lower half. She gasped to see his proud cock rearing up from the base of his flat stomach, the shaft a thick wand of dark rose while the tip shone a paler pink, glistening with love-dew. A series of mini-spasms in her vagina had her doubled up in ecstasy for a few seconds, just at the sight of him. She could feel the aching need in her vagina, which felt unbearably hollow and empty. Her hands reached out to pull him in, like a blind soul seeking the light.

But Romero had other ideas. Smiling with lustful intent, he bent his head down between her thighs again and soon she felt the deliciously cool touch of his lips parting her labia. She spread her legs wide and allowed him closer access, exulting in the giddying sensations as the flat of his tongue worked its way all over the tender convolutions of her vulva until the tip of his tongue homed in on her clitoris.

'God, that's fantastic!' she breathed, as the tension in her throbbing nub approached a crescendo.

He obviously knew exactly what he was doing, and so did Karl. Sara's arousal redoubled as the other man's deft fingers pulled relentlessly at her already swollen nipples, alternating with caresses around the straining slopes of her breasts. His lips were everywhere: pecking at her ear lobes, sucking gently at the skin of her neck, fastening on a nipple and salving it with cool saliva. He was the only one still fully clothed, but he didn't seem to mind. All his concentration was on Sara's body, all his thoughts centred on how best to please her. It was immensely flattering to be the centre of so much intense male attention.

Like the rumble of distant thunder, Sara felt her first orgasm approaching. It came upon her slowly, gentle ripples of excitement that spread from the epicentre of her sex and gradually took over her whole body. Each long spasm of bliss seemed drawn out into infinity as Romero's clever tongue kept her dancing on the edge of fulfilment with tiny, fluttering strokes and Karl completed the circuit with his gentle lickings. Then the climax gathered force and shattered its way through all the pathways of her nerves, making her cry out with sheer abandon as Sara's sense of who and where she was became completely obliterated and, for a few seconds, she became a quivering mass of pure feeling.

Later, when the two men had her lying sandwiched between them on the spacious couch, Sara felt her self-consciousness return. She didn't know what to say, or how to behave, so she lay there in silence, listening to the relaxed breathing of her lovers and wondering why they seemed to be content to give all and take nothing. Was it to be their turn next? They had pleasured her beyond her wildest imaginings, so it would be only fair. At the thought of taking either man's prick into her, Sara felt her vagina give a little shudder of excitement and some of her stored juices ran out.

When she opened her eyes Romero was smiling at her. He rolled off the sofa and helped her up, then took her into his arms and gave her a big kiss. She felt his cock twitch against her belly and from deep within her came an answering spasm of desire.

'Would you like some more champagne?' he murmured.

Soon the three of them were sitting round companionably once more, sipping the heady wine. Romero had pulled on his pants and T-shirt, so Sara was the only one who was still naked. There was a strange air of finality about the proceedings, making her wonder whether there would be any more sex that night. The two men were talking about a party they'd been invited to at the weekend, practically ignoring her, and Sara began to feel oddly like a gooseberry as names were dropped in such an obvious way that she was sure they only wanted to impress her.

'Excuse me, I think I'll get dressed now,' she said eventually, jumping to her feet.

Part of her hoped they would prevent her, with marauding hands and demanding mouths, but the two men remained seated and involved in their conversation. Sara pulled on her clothes, feeling awkward. The mood of spontaneous hedonism that had overtaken all three of them before now seemed to have faded and the party was over.

'I think I'd better be getting back,' she said.

'Well, I hope you're feeling better than when you arrived.' Karl smiled.

Sara nodded, but she had the weirdest impression. It was as if she had availed herself of a professional service and they were checking to see if she was satisfied before presenting her with the bill. Her suspicions were further aroused when Karl went on, 'I hope you feel like showing your appreciation, darling, especially to Romero. He's a wonderful actor but he's resting just now – you know how it is.'

Sara could hardly believe it. 'I – I beg your pardon?' she stammered.

'Even a lucky lady like you can recall how it was for you before you won the lottery, I'm sure. If we've brought a little sunshine into your life, don't you think it would be appropriate to acknowledge it?'

There could be no doubt now. Sara stared at the men in dismay, her mouth dry as dust. The truth dawned that they were nothing more than a couple of gigolos! She'd been completely taken in and now she felt such a fool. But she was afraid they might turn nasty if she didn't give them anything, so she opened her purse and took out all the dollar bills she had. She had no idea how much it was, and she didn't care. All she wanted was to get out of there as quickly as possible. She practically threw the money at them and made for the door.

Outside the fresh night air hit her with exhilarating force as she went next door. She was relieved to see that there was a light on and hoped that meant that Guy was at home. Hurrying through the courtyard she made her way in and found him watching television with a glass of bourbon in his hand. To her great relief he was alone.

'Guy, oh Guy! I've had such a horrible experience!'

He looked up, bemused, then poured her a whisky. 'Here, drink this. You look like you need it.'

Sara gulped some of the liquor down and flopped onto the sofa beside him. Now she'd blurted it out like that she couldn't back out of telling him, but she didn't know how to begin or how he would take it. He pressed her to tell him and she began cautiously, still unsure about their new way of relating to each other. Would he be jealous to hear that she'd been with two other men?

He seemed not to be, however. Eager for detail, he questioned her about every aspect of the encounter but when she told him about the none-too-subtle demand for money he threw back his head and roared with laughter, much to her chagrin. 'Oh, Sara! Talk about being taken for a ride.'

'But I thought he was respectable, living in that nice place next door and everything.'

'How do you think he got it? You should have realised, my love, nothing and nobody is to be taken at face value round here. Those two girls I met, they're nothing more than high-class hookers despite all their pretensions to be starlets. It's what happens to people in L.A. They come out here with stars in their eyes and end up broke, so they start on the game just to pay the rent and it becomes a way of life.'

Sara felt naive and foolish. 'Oh God, how can I face Karl again?'

'It won't make any difference. He won't think any less of you. But you don't have to have anything more to do with him, if you don't want to.'

Guy stretched out on the sofa with his head in her lap. It was so much like old times that Sara felt tears prickle in her eyes and she downed the rest of her bourbon to stave them off.

'Can't we do something together tomorrow?' she asked, forlornly. 'Something touristy, I mean, like going to Universal or Disneyland.'

He grinned up at her. 'Of course! We're still mates, aren't we? We'll call a cab in the morning and go wherever you want. This is supposed to be the holiday of a lifetime, after all.'

Sara felt relieved and disappointed at the same time. Mates – was that all they were to be to each other from now on? But she would have him all to herself for a whole day. Maybe she should be grateful for small mercies.

Chapter Six

SARA WAS SURPRISED by how much she enjoyed Guy's company on their sightseeing tour. It was reassuring to know they were still good friends, even if their marriage seemed to be going through a rocky patch. She wasn't quite ready to believe that divorce was inevitable, but she knew it would be unrealistic to expect everything to return to normal now that their lives had changed so radically. Determined to put her life on hold for the time they were on holiday, she threw herself into the kind of razzmatazz entertainment that Americans do so well.

Unable to choose which attraction to visit first, they tossed a nickel and Disneyland won. They rode around on the little train, sipped mint juleps in New Orleans Square, braved the Pirates of the Caribbean, toured the lake on the paddle steamer and had their thrills on Big Thunder Mountain. Guy entered into the spirit of it all like a big kid and, in the evening, after they'd watched a fantastic sound and light show on the lake, they made their way back to the vast, but elegant, hotel where they'd reserved a room for the night.

It was then, over their evening meal, that Sara

started to have dismal thoughts again. She noticed Guy's eyes fixed on various smartly dressed women in the restaurant and thought, He doesn't want to be with me. He'd rather find some other woman to spend the night with.

Guy noticed her sombre mood and told her to cheer up. 'We're in Disneyland, for God's sake. We're millionaires, and we're on holiday. What more do you want?'

'You,' she replied, automatically.

'You've got me.'

'You know what I mean, Guy. I want things to be like they used to be between us.'

He sighed, and she saw the frown lines on his forehead deepen. 'I don't want to hurt you, Sara. But these past few days I've been discovering things about myself. Things I never realised before.'

Sara's curiosity was instantly aroused. 'What kinds of things?'

He looked vaguely embarrassed. 'Not things I can discuss over the dinner table, that's for sure.'

'Later, then?'

Maybe. Now get your teeth into that gorgeous-looking pecan pie and lighten up, will you, woman?'

Sara smiled, but her heart was filled with foreboding. What dark secrets was he going to reveal about himself? She remembered a friend of hers whose husband had announced that he was gay after they'd had two children. Was she in for a shock like that?

After a drink at the bar they went up in the lift to the top floor of the hotel, from where they could view the floodlit towers and spires of the Sleeping

Beauty Castle in the distance. They'd chosen an expensive suite at the hotel and it was nice to sink into luxury again. 'I could get used to this.' Sara grinned at Guy as she wallowed on the huge, old-fashioned bed with its lace-trimmed canopy, crisp sheets and frilled pillows.

He came towards her with a strange look on his face and his hands behind his back. Suddenly he produced a pair of handcuffs with a flourish and dangled them before her. 'But could you get used to *this*?'

She shrank from him, remembering the way he'd rough-handled her back at the villa just a couple of nights ago. Had he turned into a raving sadist, or what?

'It's all right,' he smiled, coming to sit beside her. She noticed that the handcuffs were lined with white, soft fur. Bizarre, she thought. Her eyes widened as he reached out and stroked her cheek. He looked sad, and somehow lost. Pity for him overrode her fear as she asked him, tremulously, what this was all about.

'Those girls,' he began. 'The ones I took off with. They introduced me to things I'd only heard about vaguely, things people do to each other that I'd always thought of as kinky and weird. I didn't realise how much I wanted to do those things myself.'

'What things?'

'Oh, like being tied up, punished. Having someone dominate me.'

'Oh, I see!' Sara gave a nervous giggle of relief, pointing to the handcuffs. 'You mean these are for *you*! But you're surely not imagining that I would tie you to the bed and beat you, or anything?'

96

Guy's face fell like a disappointed child's. 'I knew you wouldn't understand,' he muttered. 'I shouldn't have said anything.'

Sara felt instantly contrite. 'I'm sorry. I was just surprised, that's all. I mean, you've never suggested anything remotely like that before.'

'I was afraid to. But I used to fantasise about it. I wanted to share my secret with you, but I didn't dare. With Sharna and Yvonne it was easy. They knew exactly what I wanted and how to give it to me. It was fantastic!'

Sara felt a hot excitement welling up inside her. The thought of Guy with those two call girls was turning her on and her curiosity was eating her up. She tried not to sound too eager as she asked, 'What did they do, then?'

Guy's expression turned shifty, his eyes sliding away from hers. 'I'm not sure I want to tell you. You might laugh at me.'

'I promise I won't,' she said, solemnly. 'Cross my heart.'

'All right.' He swung himself onto the bed beside her. It was such a large four-poster that it supported the pair of them lying side-by-side with a yard between them. Sara wanted them to be more close, to take him into her arms, but he just lay there with his hands on his chest and the incongruous restraints at his side. Sara stole quick glances at the fluffy handcuffs, wondering how and why anyone could get turned on wearing them.

'We went to this hotel, in downtown L.A.,' he began. 'It was a seedy kind of place, but it had a certain glamour. Like somewhere you'd see in the movies. I had no idea what I was in for when they suggested a three-in-a-bed scene.'

Sara flushed, remembering her own. She was still smarting under the indignity of having had to pay for sex, but Guy didn't seem to mind. At least his had been upfront, all part of the package from the start. 'Did they ask you what you wanted?'

He frowned. 'No. Somehow they seemed to guess. I suppose you must get a sixth sense for what men want if you're in their business. Anyway, they asked me if I wanted to watch the pair of them making love to each other. I'd never seen lesbians at it before – not in real life, anyway – and the idea of it turned me on a treat, so I agreed.'

Sara sat in frozen suspense, wondering what to make of it. The man she thought she knew seemed to have vanished into thin air and this stranger had taken his place. Yet she couldn't deny that she was fascinated by what he had to tell her.

'When I said yes, Sharna – she was the one with long blonde hair, big breasts and a fabulous tan – she whispered to Yvonne, but loud enough for me to hear, that she didn't want any man interfering in their sex-play and perhaps it would be best if he – meaning me – were restrained.'

'What did that make you feel?'

'Excited!' He grinned. 'And pretty horny. I thought I would come in my pants at the very idea. Sharna whipped out the handcuffs and Yvonne came over to the bed and pinned me down. She was a hefty lass. I pretended to struggle a bit, just for appearance's sake, you know. They clapped these things on my wrists and fastened me with a chain to the bedpost. Then they stripped me.'

'How? I mean – how exactly did they strip you, fast or slow?'

'Very slowly. And all the while they were talking about me as if I wasn't there, it was very strange. Yvonne said something like, "Do you think he's ready for this?" and then Sharna said, "Feel how stiff he is – of course he's ready!" It was all quite matter-of-fact, as if they were nurses talking about a patient while they gave him a bed bath or something.'

'And it excited you?'

'I'll say! When they had me naked, they pulled my feet apart and tied my ankles to the bottom of the bed with leather thongs. I felt really vulnerable and scared, I can tell you. I started to think about all those horror movies I'd seen, and poor old John Wayne Bobbitt wasn't far from my thoughts, either. What if they were some man-hating feminists, I thought, who wanted to take their revenge in some horrible way for what had been done to them?'

'Poor Guy! Did you go on being scared?'

'No, not for long. After a bit they left me alone. They seemed more interested in each other than in me. Sharna lay down on a couch in the corner – I could see it quite clearly from the bed – and Yvonne started taking the pins out of her hair. She had lovely long, dark-brown hair and a fringe. I wanted to touch her hair, only of course I couldn't.'

'Did they start making love to each other straight away?'

'They took their time. It was obvious that Yvonne was the dominant one. She began to massage Sharna's forehead and then she moved down her neck to where I could see the top of her cleavage. She was wearing quite a low-necked dress, very short, and I was longing to see what she looked like under her clothes. When Yvonne pulled down her friend's straps and showed me that she wasn't wearing a bra I felt my cock jerk up like a startled animal.'

'What did they say when they saw your erection?'

'Nothing, at first: they were so absorbed in each other. Yvonne was caressing Sharna's naked breasts. She had huge, dark pink nipples and they were straining on top of her tits. I thought she might have had silicone tits, they were so big and firm. They stood out from her chest like a pair of ... well, I can't say melons, because they weren't that shape. They were round as footballs – the English kind, of course.'

Sara sighed. She was beginning to feel like inadequate. 'You always did like big ones,' she said sullenly. The way Guy had commented on other women had always used to make her feel like that.

'Yours are nice enough,' he said graciously, before continuing. 'Well, Sharna was getting more and more worked up, with her dress bunched up around her waist, and I could see that she was touching herself down below. Yvonne saw, too. "You don't want to do that," she said. "I'll do that for you." Then she pulled down her friend's panties so I could see her brown furry pussy. It looked wonderful, even from a distance, all soft and pink and juicy. I was starting to feel extremely frustrated at this "look-but-don't-touch" game. I accused them of tormenting me. They said I didn't know what tormenting meant, and they could do it much better than that. I started to feel scared again, then.'

'How did you feel, being all tied up? Did you want them to free you?'

'That was the strange part about it; I did and I didn't. The more they went on with their love-making, the more aroused I became, but I couldn't do anything. You'd think that would make me feel really bad, but I kind of liked it. I just had to be a voyeur, you see.'

'You could have closed your eyes.'

He laughed. 'But if they'd wanted that, they could have blindfolded me, couldn't they? When Yvonne started to lick Sharna's pussy, I thought I couldn't stand it any longer. My cock was the biggest it had ever been, and when I looked down at it, the thing was so red and angry-looking, more or less the way I felt. I had to just sit there and watch while Sharna had her climax, with her hands grasping at her tits the way my hands were longing to do, and Yvonne tonguing her the way I wanted to. Talk about frustrating!'

'But I don't see the point. If they were call girls, didn't they want you to have all the fun, not them?'

'That's what I was starting to think, but I didn't know how these things work. It was all part of their plan, you see. Suddenly Yvonne looked across at me and shrieked. She said something like, "Just look at that wicked, dirty boy! See how aroused he is by watching us!" They both came over to the bed and stood looking down at my erection with a disgusted expression. I started to tremble, I was so wound up and afraid at the same time. Then they began to talk about me again as if I wasn't there.'

'What did they say?'

'Sharna said I ought to be punished for letting my feelings get the better of me. They unclipped the handcuffs and made me kneel on all fours on the bed, then they talked about how many strokes they should give me. I was that naive, I thought they meant caresses and my cock swelled even more at the thought of them stroking my bare bottom. But of course they were talking about smacking me.'

'Smacking? With their hands, you mean?'

'Yes, with their palms. They decided to alternate: first Yvonne would slap my left buttock then Sharna would slap my right one. They were very good at it, getting a rhythm up and matching the force of the blows so it felt almost as if the same person were doing it. At first I felt really stupid and I wanted to ask them to stop, but soon my bottom felt all warm and tingly and I began to like it.'

'They didn't hurt you, then?'

'Not too much. I felt like the naughty little boy they were pretending I was, and I rather liked that. My cock liked it too. I kept my erection all through their punishment routine.'

Sara grinned. She was quite enjoying the thought of the two women belabouring him. If she'd known that was what he was in for, she might not have minded him going off with them quite so much.

'What did they think of that?'

'They pretended not to like it at all. "That hasn't worked," Sharna said, and this time she actually felt my cock. "His erection is as strong as ever." So then Yvonne said, "Do you know how to make it go down?" and Sharna said she did. I was trem-

102

bling all over by now and bright red. I'd never have believed that having those women talking about me like that, and handling my prick as if it were a piece of meat, could be such a turn-on.'

'What did Sharna say, then?'

'She said my erection would probably subside if she let it go where it wanted to go. I thought she meant into her pussy, and I was all keyed up waiting for that. But then she said it was aiming straight at her tits, which was true, so she would cuddle it and soothe it between her breasts and that would make it go to sleep. She talked about my cock as if it were a baby, would you believe? You can imagine how I felt then. I couldn't wait!'

Sara had heard about tit-wanking, but had never felt inspired to try it herself. A pang of envy assailed her when she thought of Guy's penis nestling in Sharna's cleavage. She could see he was turned on by the idea even now as his cock reared impatiently; she put out her hand to feel it.

'Not now,' Guy said, sharply. 'Let me finish. I wanted to tell you what happened next. As soon as Sharna got onto all fours with my cock between her boobs, Yvonne came wriggling round the back and started to lick her from behind. So while Sharna was massaging my cock with her huge breasts she was getting her share too. I could see Yvonne slavering all over her buttocks and pushing her fingers into her, making Sharna wiggle and moan. My cock was burning, throbbing like an overheated engine as it wallowed in all that firm, satiny flesh and my eyes were goggling at the sight of what Yvonne was doing to her. I kept trying to work it out as she chopped and changed. Eventually I realised that she was licking her in front while she put her finger in her arse, so Sharna was getting it both ways. The minute I sussed that out I came all over her boobs; my climax was so violent, I thought I would injure myself.'

Sara was feeling quite randy now, but she didn't know what to say to Guy. His confession had been very titillating, but now that it was over, she felt embarrassed on his behalf. It sounded as if he had let the two tarts use and abuse him while he revelled in the whole thing. That didn't seem like the Guy she knew, who had always wanted to be in charge – in bed and out.

'Have I shocked you?' he inquired, softly.

'No! I'm just surprised that you would like that sort of thing.'

'I was surprised, too, but the fact remains I found it enormously satisfying. I've been puzzling over it ever since, wondering why I was so into it. Then I remembered that teenage girl, Janie. I think I told you about her.'

'The one who used to baby-sit, when you were about eight or nine?'

'That's her. She used to come in and watch me when I had my bath. Sometimes I used to splash around a bit too much for her liking, and then she'd put me across her knee and spank my bare, wet bottom. I can remember the smell of her, and the feel of her breasts as she bent over me. I also remember it giving me erections. I think it all stems from that.'

'Probably.'

Guy reached out for her and drew her into his arms. Sara snuggled up, feeling reassured. He still had a stiff penis beneath his trousers and she was half-tempted to touch it, but thought better of it. So much had changed between them, and so quickly, that she felt quite unsure of her feelings. With the memory of her threesome still fresh, she felt uneasy, wondering if he expected a confession from her in exchange. If he did, he wasn't going to get one.

He kissed her and murmured something in her ear. She didn't hear him properly the first time and he had to repeat it. 'Will you put the cuffs on me?'

She raised herself up and stared down at him in bewilderment. 'Why?'

He gave a weird smile. 'Because I like it.'

'But what else do you want me to do? I'm not going to beat you, if that's what you think.'

'No, I don't expect that. Just put them on me and let me look at you.'

She shrugged, but could see no harm in it. There was something exciting in the idea of having him at her mercy, even though she had no intention of abusing her power over him. She picked up the handcuffs and examined them, her fingertips touching the soft fur lining. Then she opened them up and clasped them around his wrists. 'Where's the key?'

'In my trouser pocket. Don't worry, you'll be able to undo them.'

'I hope so, or it could be embarrassing.'

'I won't embarrass you.'

His hands were clasped in front of him, but Sara could see his erection bulging beneath his fly. All this talk had evidently got him going, or was it just having the handcuffs on?

'Will you do something more for me?' he asked her, his tone faintly wheedling.

'Depends what it is.'

105

'Strip for me.'

She laughed. 'What good would that do you? You've seen it all before.'

'I know, but not . . . like this. Please?'

Sara stared at him, not knowing what to make of his request. Of course she would have to undress to get into bed, but was he asking her to do a striptease for him, to get him even more aroused? She hesitated, looking into his dark, unfathomable eyes. How far they had come since winning the lottery! She felt both apart from him and a part of him, still.

'Will you just do it for me, Sara?'

His voice teetered on the edge of pleading. Sara still didn't know what to make of it. This seemed like a game of cat and mouse, but who was the cat and who was the mouse? Slowly she rose and walked across the thick pile of the cream carpet in her stockinged feet. She was acutely aware that he was watching her, and equally aware of the power she had over him. Only when he'd asked her to marry him had she felt this same heady certainty that if she refused him he would be shattered.

Turning, she gave him a shy smile. Then, deciding to make the best of it, she tossed back her hair like a Spanish dancer and slipped one strap of her dress down her shoulder. Guy moaned a little, shifting further up onto the pillow to get a better view. His eyes were glazed and distant, as if he'd entered some fantasy world of his own making, and Sara wondered how many times he had been in that same world while making love to her.

The thought made her angry, and she pulled down the zipper of her dress and stepped out of it almost contemptuously, waving it around as she'd seen girls do on film, and throwing it on the floor. Clad only in her push-up bra and panties, a slim suspender belt holding up her sleek, pearl-grey stockings, she pirouetted to display herself and made some suggestive thrusts with her pelvis. She had intended the whole thing to be a send-up, but the effect on her was oddly exciting. Guy's penis was like a beacon to her, its stiff stalk and burning tip egging her on.

Sensing that her very anger was arousing Guy, Sara made her act even more menacing by strutting around and flashing demonic glances in his direction. He was lapping it up. A faint smile of satisfaction confirmed what she saw in his eyes, that his imagination had transfommed her into some kind of sex vixen. She began to wish that she had a whip to lash the air with. And maybe some killer heels and a cinched-in corset would help, too . . .

My God, I'm getting sucked into it, Sara realised with alarm. Yet her snarling expression never wavered and as she unhooked her bra-cups from her breasts she felt a distinct twinge of dark, dirty desire. If she *had* a whip she could actually envisage using it on him. The thought disturbed her. She found herself absently clutching at her breasts, stimulating her nipples with her thumbs and suddenly Guy cried out, 'Yes! More of that, please!'

'More of what?' she asked, out of character.

His voice was guttural as he replied, 'What you're doing to your breasts. I want to see you pleasure yourself. I want to watch you come.'

This was not the Guy she knew. A year ago the notion that he would be content to watch her masturbate instead of doing it for her himself would have seemed absurd. And as for being handcuffed . . . ! But since then, they had won the lottery, and now they were no longer the same people. If a temporary madness had overtaken them, there was no wonder that it was manifesting in their sex life. Even so, such sudden changes were hard to take.

Sara pulled an elegant little chair towards her and sat down, spreading her thighs wide. Still caressing her breasts with her left hand, she used her right to rub her swollen labia through the thin cotton of her underwear. Responding instantly to the stimulation, her clitoris stood proud from its hood and she could feel the hard little nub throbbing wildly as she pressed her fingers into the hot cushion of flesh.

Soon she was caught up in the need to climax, her fingers busy at both hot spots, coaxing more and more sensation out of her inflamed body. Intermittently aware of her husband's groans, Sara scarcely heeded him as she squirmed and thrust her way towards orgasm. When she did glance in his direction it was to see him straining helplessly while his cock danced before both their eyes like a mocking jester, ridiculous in its puffed-up pride.

A sense of triumph overcame her, together with a feeling of her own strength. It poured from her in a wave of blissful energy, giving her once again the thrill of omnipotence, of limitless possibilities, that she'd felt when the reality of winning the lottery had come home to her. Slowly the overwhelming feelings subsided, leaving her spent and breathless, needing to lie down. She staggered over to the bed and collapsed beside Guy, ignoring him.

But then she heard his urgent whisper, 'Beat me, Sara!'

Opening bleary eyes she stared up at him, uncertain of what she had heard. Again he pleaded, 'I want you to beat me.'

He got up awkwardly onto his knees and she saw the crying need in his erection. Then he bent over, exposing his backside to her in confirmation of his request. Wearily, Sara got to her knees and raised her hand to the task. She slapped him feebly at first, feeling the slack buttocks give beneath her palm, but as she regained her strength the blows became more forceful and his buttocks grew firm, offering more resistance. Energised by the action, she began to get into a stinging rhythm that punished her palms as well as his behind.

Suddenly Guy collapsed with a loud groan and she realised that her mission was accomplished and he was spilling his seed onto the bed. A wave of disgust threatened to overtake her, but she resisted it and went into the bathroom to take a shower. She covered herself from head to foot in *Giorgio Aire* then let the stream of warm water wash it all off, leaving her fresh and invigorated.

Too perked up to sleep, Sara sprawled in a huge tub of an armchair watching television while Guy snored noisily on the bed. She didn't want to think about what had happened. The mindless soaps and unfamiliar advertisements of American TV served her purpose in obliterating all reflection and, after half an hour of mind-numbing viewing, she felt ready for sleep.

After slipping in beside Guy she turned out the bedside light and lay in darkness, but then the thoughts came crowding back and her mind was in turmoil once more. What if she was expected to go on doing that sort of thing for him? What if his requests became more and more bizarre? Was she willing to put up with his quirky tastes to save their marriage? The memory of how she had half-enjoyed it returned to taunt her. But was that the kind of relationship she wanted with the main man in her life?

Confused and upset, Sara turned her back on her husband and vowed not to think about it again until the morning.

Chapter Seven

GUY WAS VERY good to Sara for the next few days. He took her to smart Rodeo Drive and encouraged her to buy any designer clothes that took her fancy. He bought her lavish dinners in the best restaurants, where they could enjoy star-spotting, and together they toured the film studios, Universal and Warner. At night he made no special demands on her, sensing perhaps that he had gone too far before, but he made no attempt to seek out other women and when they made love he was tender and considerate, just the way he'd been when they were first married. So Sara began to relax, thinking there was hope for them after all.

One morning when they were lazing at the villa, Karl suddenly appeared on the beach next door and called a greeting. 'Hi, Sara. Aren't you going to introduce me to your husband?'

She was instantly flustered. After the embarrassment of that threesome, she had been giving their neighbour a wide berth, but there was no way she could wriggle out of this one with dignity. Resignedly, Sara took Guy up to the screen of shrubs that divided the properties and introduced the two men. They shook hands in a friendly manner and were soon chatting amiably. Sara relaxed as she saw her husband come under the other man's spell.

But then Karl uttered words that filled her with panic. 'A friend of mine is having a barbecue tonight. Why don't you both come along? You'd meet some great folks, and have a fabulous time. That's guaranteed.'

His blue eyes were sparkling with good humour but Sara was suspicious. She thought she knew who his friend was – the woman on the beach – and what kind of good time he had in mind, but there was no way she could warn Guy.

Warn him? She smiled ironically at her own naivety. He'd probably lap it all up. Hearing her husband's enthusiastic acceptance she knew that she would either have to go along with it, make some excuse, or tell him the truth about Karl and his coterie. She felt angry that this dilemma had been sprung on her just when things had started to settle down between her and Guy, but there was nothing she could do about it now.

Sara's suspicions were further aroused when Guy said she should buy something special to wear for the barbecue. She had seen him talking to Karl in the afternoon and watched them continue their animated conversation as they strolled along the beach together. Was Guy now fully informed about the kind of company their neighbour kept?

'I've got plenty to choose from already,' she said with sullen insistence when he began to talk about going downtown. 'I don't need to buy anything new.'

'But all your dresses are so ... I don't know. They're lovely dresses, darling, don't get me wrong. But they're awfully formal for a barbecue.'

'What do you suggest then – shorts and a T-shirt? I've plenty of those, too.'

'Mm . . . I don't know. It's something I'll know when I see it. Karl recommended this little boutique.'

'Ah, Karl. I might have known he'd have something to do with it.'

Guy bridled. 'I don't know what you mean. Surely he's the best person to advise on what to wear for his friend's party?'

'He's got some pretty weird friends. I should imagine it will be like fancy dress.'

But she realised at once that she'd fallen into a trap. Guy's grin widened. 'In that case, it's all the more important for us to look right. I'll ring for a cab. It won't take us more than an hour or two, then we can come back for a rest before we get ready.'

By the time they arrived at the place Karl recommended Sara had resigned herself to spending more money on some outlandish outfit, but her head spun as she walked through the door into a wonderland of bizarre fetish gear. The shop was called On the Wild Side and that described its merchandise exactly. The place was awash with leather and vinyl, silk, velvet and fur. Much of it was black but there were some strong colours, too: turquoise, pink and red. The garments ranged from voluptuous-looking corsets to heavy bondage gear, all zippers, chains and straps.

The fat transvestite who ran the place and introduced herself as Mariella became quite ingratiating when Guy mentioned why Karl had sent them.

'So, you got an invite to Angelina's barbie?' she

cooed, her dark eyes gleaming with appetite. 'Lucky guys! There are some of us who would trade whole body parts to get such an invite. Mind you, I'm not saying which part.'

There was something about this camp old queen that made Sara's heart soften towards her. Mariella grew quite excited as she began to assess her potential. 'You've got a lovely figure, sweetie. I see you in purple, yes definitely, with black patent and maybe a touch of pink. Come over here, darling, and let's see what I can find for you.'

She started to pull out several items ranging, in Sara's eyes, from the ridiculous to the absurd. Try as she might she simply couldn't see herself in a leopard-print bustier with matching stockings and dog collar, or a tasselled fishnet body stocking, or a pink leather, plunge-fronted teddy laced across the bust with chains.

'How about this?' Mariella suggested at last, her tone a trifle exasperated.

The garment she held out for Sara's inspection was a red latex bikini trimmed with white marabou feathers. It was pretty and tempting, just the thing to show off her newly acquired tan. She examined the cups, wondering if they were her size, and discovered that there was a flap over the nipples that could be worn open or closed.

'Go for it,' Guy encouraged her, evidently tired of waiting.

'May I suggest one or two accessories?' Mariella said, searching amongst her racks. 'These sandals, for instance.' She held up a pair of shiny red patent sandals with impossibly high heels.

'I couldn't wear those,' Sara gasped. 'I'd break my ankle.'

'How about these, then?'

Although the shiny red bootees had lower heels, they had very pointed toes. Eventually Sara chose a pair of lower-heeled white sandals with crisscross ties that went up to her knee, giving the impression of open-laced boots. Mariella suggested a set of white fur cuffs and collar, too. 'You'll look like Mrs Claus, dear!'

At first Sara didn't understand. 'Claws?' she repeated, thinking pussy.

Mariella gave a theatrical toss of her huge black wig. 'Wife of that bitch Santa, who only rewards goody-goodies.'

Sara laughed and went off into a nearby cubicle to try on the clothes, out of sight of passers-by. The bra was very clingy, making her breasts feel hot and tight, but she loved the way her nipples protruded through the thin red latex like a pair of glacé cherries. When she slipped on the briefs the soft material slipped right into her crotch, stimulating her clitoris with its bandage-tight effect. No wonder people like wearing this stuff, she thought. Bending over to lace up her sandals was the equivalent of foreplay, with the strip of latex pressed hard into her vulva and her breasts almost bursting out of the skintight cups. She put on the accessories and made her entrance back into the shop.

'Oh darling, you look wonderful,' Mariella crowed. Guy was speechless, but his eyes were wallowing in every detail of her appearance.

'I'm going to be terribly hot and sweaty in this,' Sara protested.

Mariella gave her a brief peck on the cheek, enveloping her in some heady perfume that was obviously intended to hide other, less feminine, odours. 'Well, you know that wonderful old saying? "Horses sweat, men perspire, but ladies merely glow." You will glow beautifully, my dear.'

'You look great, Sara,' Guy offered.

'And now how about you?' Mariella said, giving him all her attention. 'We have some wonderful bondage trousers that would suit you down to a T.'

Guy looked startled. He'd evidently not imagined himself wearing any such thing. Sara stifled a giggle and then said, 'Oh, you must – or you'd look quite out of place next to me.'

Guy flushed beetroot as Mariella presented him with a series of outrageous garments involving leather, straps, studs and chains. 'If you've got a Prince Albert you can use this chain as a tether,' she said, with a coy grin. 'Then you can put your watch on the other end and keep it in your pocket.'

Sara was mystified, but Guy promised to explain later. He was toying with the idea of a pair of black lederhosen, held up by chain-braces and Mariella suggested he should try them on. She produced matching high boots, anklets, cuffs and a studded dog collar but he said he didn't want to wear the full Monty. He went off while Sara got out of her things and Mariella wrapped them up for her.

When Guy reappeared, Sara was staggered by the change in his appearance. Instead of the fairly good-looking but ordinary young man she had married, there was a self-conscious but very ambivalent-looking slave. Even without the additional restraints, Guy had every appearance of one born to serve. The little leather trousers gave him a naughty schoolboy look but the chains that divided his tanned chest into neat strips suggested

116

something far more submissive. In addition the tiny black leather boots he had chosen to wear, with their cowboy style and high heels, were so camp that he looked as if he'd walked straight out of a gay bar.

'How do I look?' he asked, uncertainly, looking straight at Sara.

She was struggling to keep the corners of her mouth, which were threatening to spread into a wide grin, firmly in place. 'Very good. I'm sure we'll knock 'em dead, the pair of us.'

'You'll be the belles of the ball, my lovelies.' Mariella smiled. 'Or should that be the balls of the . . . oh, never mind! Now I'm sorry to have to introduce the d-word, but filthy lucre will rear its ugly head sooner or later in this temple of Mammon. How are we going to secure our goodies, may I ask?'

Guy flashed his gold card and Mariella took it greedily. 'They say all that glitters is not gold, but this is a very good imitation,' she quipped. 'I'll be right back.'

Sara was relieved when they emerged into the sunshine again, with boxes and packets under their arms. 'Whew, that was some boutique,' Guy exclaimed, as he hailed a cab. 'Makes me wonder what this barbecue is going to be like. Do you think we'll blend in, wearing this weird gear?'

'I don't think we'd blend without it,' Sara said wryly, bending to get into the cab.

There was time for a short siesta when they got back to the villa. Sara hung her red bikini on a hanger and lay on the bed examining it at a distance. It did look rather Christmassy, but why not? Just lately she'd worn all kinds of clothes that

117

she would never have worn before.

Suddenly it occurred to her that she simply didn't care what people thought of her any more. It was a revelation. Having money meant that to a large extent she could wear what she liked, act how she liked, do what she liked and say what she liked. She was no longer afraid of losing her job, offending the neighbours, making the wrong impression, or any of those constraints that kept ordinary people in line. Wasn't that what Guy had been driving at when he'd said, 'What's the point of having loads if you can't do as you like?'

Guy came out of the shower looking all steamy and delicious and, for a moment, Sara desired him desperately. Then her heart sank. They were going to this party together, but the chances were that they would not come home as a couple. If Guy had meant what he said about being free to follow his dick, then he would be after someone new and, from what Karl had intimated, there would be plenty of delectable female flesh on show that evening.

But, by the same token, there should be some attractive males. Sara tried to work up some enthusiasm for the prospect of finding a new lover, but it was hard to do so in the abstract, and her experience with the two gigolos next door had rather put her off. She stood under the shower, letting its warm rain sluice off her bodily secretions, and tried her best to get into a party mood. When I've had a couple of drinks it will be easier, she told herself.

They rang a cab to collect them at nine and when the driver saw their strange clothes he knew at once where they were bound.

'Don't tell me, you want Angelina's place – am I right, or am I right? They call her the Queen Angel – don't ask me why. Those people who don't like her, they call her the Queer Angel. But they're the ones who don't get invited. Soon as they get invited again, she's back on her throne. Don't ask me why. I don't move in those circles. If I did, I wouldn't be sitting in the driver's seat of this lousy cab, I'd be in the back like you. But sometimes I reckon it's safer to be in the driver's seat, you know what I mean? You get to see what's up ahead. Some of those cookies she gets at her parties, they don't know which goddamn bed they're gonna wake up in tomorrow. They got no idea what's up ahead for them. AIDS, hepatitis A, B, all the letters of the alphabet, gonorrhoea, drug addiction – that's the type go to her parties. Hey, you sure you don't wanna go someplace else? I could turn around right now, take you back to L.A. I know a real nice little bar where you could have a cocktail, somethin' good to eat, listen to some sweet music. You look like a nice couple, know what I mean . . .'

Sara listened to his tirade with increasing trepidation but Guy simply found it all highly amusing. The man continued in the same vein all the way along Highway 1 until they reached the villa where Karl's friend lived. She remembered the entrance, but nothing else about the place was familiar. Lights were strung all along the drive, swaying slightly in the breezy night air, and there were more lights in the grounds where small round tables had been set up. Live music drifted around, now loud and now soft as the wind changed direction, and there was a concentration of light on the distant beach where the main action seemed to be taking place. Guy paid the driver, who took his leave of them as if he never expected them to leave the place alive, and then they began to walk across the manicured lawn towards the steps that led down the cliff.

It was quite chilly now the sun had gone down and Sara was glad of the blue velvet cloak she had slung around her shoulders at the last minute before leaving the villa. She hugged its comforting warmth close across her chest, clinging to Guy's arm as they made their way gingerly down the steps. It occurred to her that unless they met up with Karl they would know absolutely nobody there. What if they were challenged; would they be thrown out as gate-crashers? She only had a few dollars and her gold card secreted in the inside pocket of her cloak, and she knew that Guy didn't have much more on him.

Then the words of the cabbie rang ominously in Sara's ears as she saw the huge throng of people gathered on the beach around a ring of barbecues: 'That dame's got connections, know what I mean? With the Big M.'

At first Sara couldn't recognise Angelina amongst the crowd of weirdly dressed people that was milling around the barbecues or dancing on the beach to the strains of a rock band. She couldn't see Karl either, and as they approached the party her fears of rejection were doubled. The latex costume was working its way into her vulva as she walked, making her feel both aroused and vulnerable. She wasn't used to feeling so horny in the company of strangers. To add to her disquiet there were some heavy guys in full leather kit standing

120

around and she was sure they were bouncers.

Then someone with blonde cropped hair who appeared to be naked turned around and Sara recognised the gleam in those mocking green eyes. But that was a man, surely? Yet there was something not quite right. In the glow from the lanterns and the smoking barbecues it was difficult to recognise anyone, but she edged forward and then gave a gasp of surprise. The 'man' was a woman, even though she was completely naked! Her body had been very skilfully painted to look like a man's: her breasts covered in a mat of dark hair and her nipples made smaller, while a permanently erect organ was delineated on her stomach, rising from her mat of pubic curls. Close to, it was obvious, but from a distance it had looked disturbingly realistic.

And it was Angelina; Sara was sure of it now.

The strange apparition approached, no doubt drawn by Sara's gob-smacked expression.

'Welcome, friends.' She smiled. 'I don't believe we've been introduced?'

There was just a hint of menace in her deep voice, and Sara knew that they must make the right response or they'd be out on their ear. 'Karl invited us,' she said at once. 'He's our neighbour. He sent us to Wild Side to get kitted out.'

'Yes, I thought I recognised our Mariella's vulgar taste.' She turned and called into the crowd. 'Karl! Your friends are here. Come and take care of them, darling, they know no one.'

She drifted off, but as Karl separated himself from the crowd Sara was aware of various eyes swivelling towards them, making sure they were who they claimed to be. She forced a smile as Karl came up to them wearing a frogman's outfit. No wonder she hadn't recognised him. He lumbered up to them and removed his mouthpiece so that he could speak.

I don't believe I'm really here, with these people dressed like this, Sara told herself, tempted to pinch her own arm just to make sure she wasn't dreaming.

'Hi! Welcome to the party. You look fantastic, both of you.' He kissed both of them on the cheek, much to Guy's embarrassment. 'There's some folks over here who would love to meet you. They just adore English people.'

Sara prayed that Romero would not be among them.

The people that Karl introduced them to were all naked except for manacles, cuffs and body jewellery. There was a black woman with enormous bouncing breasts and pierced nipples, a Chinese man with kung fu muscles, a Latino type and an androgynous blonde with tiny pert breasts and boyish hips. They looked like exotic slaves at an auction. Sara and Guy were welcomed enthusiastically, but as the conversation proceeded it became obvious that Karl had described them as 'English millionaires' which, to the Americans, meant that they must also be titled. Unwilling to confess that they'd won their wealth, Sara kept trying to insist that she wasn't Lady anyone but when they insisted on addressing Guy as 'Milord', she realised that she was being taken for his mistress, which riled her – especially as her husband seemed to be lapping up his new title and had no intention of disillusioning them.

After a few glasses of champagne, Sara began to

succumb to a devil-may-care mood. She was in a state of permanent arousal now, her pussy throbbing beneath the tight latex band that was pressing hard against her clitoris and her nipples stimulated by the bra whenever she moved her arms. She noticed that the party was becoming more swinging with couples, threesomes and foursomes slipping into the little tents that were dotted about all over the beach and which Karl coyly referred to as 'love pavilions'. There were other couples who didn't seem to mind being watched. Sara could see them performing in the shadows surrounded by spectators who chewed on chicken legs, munched sausages and swigged beer just as if they were at a ball game.

Feeling curiously detached from it all, Sara decided to go on a tour of exploration. She left her husband and wandered through the crowd, attracting attention as she went. Sometimes hands would reach out and give her breasts or bottom a pinch or a caress, or someone would kiss her cheek. One woman, dressed entirely in black leather, came up and kissed her rapaciously on the mouth, asking Sara if she wanted to join her 'chain gang'. Sara gracefully declined and the woman gave a theatrical little pout, then disappeared into a nearby tent.

After a while, Sara felt peckish and approached one of the barbecues to get herself a plate of ribs and salad. She spread the blue cloak over the bank of cushions then settled down to watch the lights reflected on the ocean. It felt good to be alone for a few minutes, but she wasn't that way for long. Two figures made a beeline for the cushions and asked if they could join her. Sara looked up at two of the most gorgeous human beings she had ever seen. They were very alike and could almost have been twins, although they could have achieved the similarities in their appearance by other means.

The man was blond and blue-eyed, but not at all like Karl. His hair was shoulder-length and attractively tousled. His face was very pure and boyish, almost angelic, and his body was smooth and hairless. He wore only a chamois loincloth and strappy sandals, his skin honey-toned, and he showed none of the overdeveloped musculature that so many of the men there seemed to possess. But he oozed sex from every pore and, when he smiled, his teeth formed a perfect white arc between smooth, kissable lips.

Reluctantly Sara diverted her gaze towards his companion: a girl with similar hair, eyes and skin tone. She was a few inches shorter, however, and her breasts were eye-catching, exquisitely round and full with large pink nipples playing peekaboo through the long fringe of her chamois-leather bikini top. Down below she wore a demure fringed apron over her sex.

'Hi,' Sara gulped, 'do sit down. I was enjoying the ocean. Doesn't it look beautiful, with all the lights on it?'

To her surprise, the pair positioned themselves either side of her and, without saying a word, took her almost empty plate and set it down on the sand out of the way. Then they began to kiss her lightly on both cheeks. Their lips were petal-soft as they pressed against her face and nibbled gently at her ear lobes. Sara sat completely still, unsure how to handle it, but her body was keyed up with excitement. She could smell the alluring perfume that the couple wore and feel their warm bodies brush against hers.

Soon they were touching her with their hands too, stroking her thighs and upper arms, filling her with bright, hot energy. Beneath her latex bikini she could feel her flesh straining for release and the effect was gratifying. The tight garments were helping to raise her temperature and soon as she was covered all over by a light film of sweat.

The couple were working in complete synchronicity, each attending to the same spot on either side of her body. When the boy kissed her right cheek the girl kissed the left, and the same with her ears, her neck, her shoulders. As soon as she realised that they were working their way right down her body in tandem, Sara gave a low moan of suppressed lust and lay back against the cushions in a state of anticipatory bliss, more than happy to let them get on with it.

They reached her breasts and slowly worked their way into the tight cups of her bikini until they could reach her erect, tingling nipples. Their tongues were perfectly attuned, each lapping and softly sucking with the same style, and Sara gave herself up completely to the novelty of experiencing perfectly symmetrical stimulation. It was as if one lover had two tongues and four hands, all working in her service, and she found it incredibly stimulating. Within the latex pouch her clitoris was yearning and swelling towards orgasm.

Slowly Sara felt the warm tongues move down past her breasts to her sensitive midriff, which was quivering with tension. Smoothly licking at her belly, as if she were good enough to eat, they began to stroke her damp thighs at the same time and the level of stimulation became excruciating. Sara moaned; she would have begged if she hadn't somehow retained a smidgin of pride. Inwardly, she was screaming at them to please, please pull down those rubber pants and find her demanding little button. She was on heat down there, tropical heat, and the sticky latex felt as if it would melt into her, melding with her flesh.

Then, at last, she felt them start to roll down the pants, revealing her matted pubic hair. Sara gasped with relief as her mound was exposed to the cool night air; she moved her thighs to allow the clingy material to be rolled down them to her knees, the stuff slapping against her with an elastic sound as it went. Her whole vulva was buzzing with erotic energy by the time she was free of the restricting garment, and then she felt soft mouths working their way up her shins, achingly slowly, past her knees and up her thighs, leaving a trail of saliva behind them that felt delicious as it cooled.

Her body tensing as she felt the tender little mouths move towards her vulva, Sara was on a knife edge, about to explode. Fingers were pressed softly into her groin while the pair of tongues carefully pushed back her labia on either side and slowly licked up the groove between the inner and outer lips. It was so exquisitely titillating that it made her squirm and moan with desire. Soon they were giving her alternate licks on the clitoris, stroking upward from root to tip and sending her into a frenzy of trembling suspense.

With one accord their hands slipped beneath her and began to squeeze her buttocks, moulding her flesh with such delicate precision that her pussy was lifted, this way and that, towards their feasting mouths. Soon they were taking it in turns to plunge their hot tongues right into her creamy quim, sucking out her juices and thrusting into her with equal enthusiasm while their lips brushed against the fiery tip of her clitoris.

Their interchange was smooth and rhythmic, expertly leading her on towards orgasm, and it didn't take long before she was there, writhing on her velvet cloak in a blissed-out state of total fulfilment while gentle hands caressed her, spreading the climax out in space and time until it saturated her senses and overwhelmed her completely.

After all that sensual excess, she sank down into the welcome relief of oblivion, her eyes closed and her pulse gradually returning to normal. Sara drifted into slumber and, when she came to, the night air was chilly on her cooled flesh; she reached out to pull the velvet cloak around her but her fingers touched the bare sand. Confused, she sat up and looked about her.

The cushions were strewn around and she was lying directly on the beach but, at first, she couldn't see her cloak. Then she noticed it, bundled up some distance away. There were no people around at all. The party seemed to have moved into the grounds, or the villa itself, and some of the little tents had toppled over. What had happened? Had there been high winds or something?

Sara got up slowly, feeling stiff, and put her bikini bottom back on with difficulty, wincing as it pulled against her tender flesh. She then adjusted the bra and staggered over to the pile of navy-blue velvet. Picking up the heavy cloak, it occurred to her to feel inside the pocket. It was empty. Frantically, she searched around the spot; she retraced her steps to where she had been lying. She threw the cushions around, thinking that her money and gold card must have dropped out while she was in full sexual spate, but there was no sign of her possessions.

Grim suspicion assailed her. She wrapped the cloak right around her and began to stride back up the beach, wondering what had become of her 'angelic' lovers. Had she been well and truly fleeced by them? It was hard to come to any other conclusion. She wondered where Guy was, too, and what he'd been up to. What a fool he would think her, when she confessed to having been duped. Perhaps she should say nothing but rely on him to pay for the cab home.

There were piles of people on the lawn behind the villa, and dim lights still shone here and there, but she couldn't see anyone she recognised. After several minutes of staggering around in semi-darkness she sank onto a bench and put her head in her hands, despairing. She was cold, tired and her head ached. All she wanted was to go home, or to what passed for home. She thought about her real home, back in England, felt a wholehearted desire to return there, to familiar surroundings. This holiday had turned sour on her . . . and where the hell was Guy?

She saw him in the small hours of the morning when she was drifting off to sleep again. He came up from the beach looking raddled, his chains clanking around his waist and his feet bare. Sara waved and he came over to her wearily, sinking onto the bench beside her. 'Hi, doll! Had a good time?'

'Have I, hell! Someone's only nicked my cash and credit card.'

'Shit!' His eyes were fully open now. 'Any idea who?'

She nodded, tight-lipped. 'They must have done a runner by now. Who should I phone to put a stop on the card?'

He looked dazed. 'I dunno. Look, our best bet is to get a cab and go back to the villa. I've got all the details there, somewhere.'

While they waited for the cab to arrive they sat in silence, each absorbed in their own thoughts. Guy seemed to be happy enough, although he was obviously shagged out, but Sara was silently fuming. She couldn't help thinking about that couple of 'angels' and how they had taken her in with their pretty faces and practised lovemaking. They must be laughing themselves sick over her now and there was nothing she could do about it. With a shock, she realised that she didn't even know their names.

Sara dozed in the cab but Guy took charge as soon as they got in, ringing the international helpline and finding out about getting a new credit card sent to her. But when he started to tell her about it she put up her hand.

'I don't think I want to bother, Guy. I've had enough of this so-called holiday. I want to go home. You can book me a flight on your card, can't you?'

'Well, I could, but –'

'I mean it. I want to be on the first possible flight out of L.A. tomorrow. You can stay here, if you like. There's another couple of weeks booked on the villa, and you seem to be enjoying yourself.' The words had a more bitter tinge to them than she'd intended.

Guy shrugged, but didn't try to argue. 'OK, if that's how you feel.'

'It is. And now I'm going to bed. If you're awake before me in the morning, perhaps you'd do me the favour of ringing the airport, then making sure I get to the plane on time.'

She took the spare bed in the little guest room. After stripping off the red latex bikini, she fell into the bed with a huge sigh of relief and was soon fast asleep.

Chapter Eight

THE HOUSE WAS just as they had left it, yet it looked somehow different. Sara dumped her luggage and then, jet-lagged as she was, sat in the living room looking about her and wondering where her life was going. Everything in that room had memories and associations. The vase had been a wedding present from her Auntie Joan; they'd bought the sofa together at IKEA; the carpet was second-hand and she could remember they'd gone to the house following up a small ad, the couple had been going through a divorce . . . That'll be us, soon, she thought, and a terrible bone-aching weariness settled on her.

Sara ran the answerphone and found several whining messages from Guy's mother along the lines of, 'Where are you, darling? Have you gone away? Why didn't you tell me? Please phone.' She left them on the machine. He could deal with the old bat himself. Once, she would have taken the job on, but things were different now. Bitter tears welled up as fatigue and fears for the future combined to drag her down.

After a nap she felt a bit better, and took the car to the local supermarket to stock up. It was a shock

131

to meet one of her old friends, Jenny, in the queue at the checkout.

'Hi, Sara, I've not seen you for ages. How are things?' she asked brightly. Sara had made a decision not to tell any friends or neighbours about their win. Not yet, anyway. She made vague noises and Jenny said, 'Have you been on holiday? You've got a lovely tan. Don't say you got it in your back garden.'

'It's fake,' she lied.

'Really? I wouldn't have thought you were the fake tan type. Hey, have you seen the new gallery in Hawker's Lane?'

'Gallery?'

'Yes, you know, paintings. I knew you'd been to art school so I thought you'd have seen it already. A woman with long hair runs it; she seems rather nice.' Jenny picked up her groceries. 'Sorry, love, I must dash. Simon's due out of school in . . . oh my God, five minutes!'

As Jenny dashed off, Sara felt sadness overwhelm her. It had been such a normal conversation, just the sort they used to have. But if she'd known about the win Sara doubted whether Jenny would ever have been able to act normally with her again. She felt in limbo, unable to see her old friends, yet equally unable to make new ones. There had to be some way out of the dead end she found herself in.

On the way home, she remembered the new gallery and decided to call in. Since her marriage, she'd let her interest in art slide somewhat, since Guy thought all modern art was tosh. Even the Impressionists were suspect in his book. Making a detour down Hawker's Lane, she came across the rather pretentiously named Galleria Moderna in an old, bow-fronted shop that used to be a jewellers, and walked straight in.

The paintings on show were mostly by up-and-coming young artists straight out of college, but there were a few names she recognised: Christoforo Lambini, an Italian now living in Chelsea, and Sven Haraldsen, a particular favourite of hers from the 1980s. She was examining his watercolour of a fjord when a young woman appeared from the back of the shop. Dressed in a purplish-blue smock, with her long dark hair braided into a single plait, she was clearly the owner.

'Hello.' She smiled cheerily, glancing at Sara's shopping. 'Were you just passing?'

'I only heard about this place ten minutes ago. It's really nice.'

'Thank you. We've only been here a fortnight. Are you interested in Sven's work?'

'Oh yes; I know him of old.'

After that, they chatted for the best part of an hour. The woman was called Emily, and had been to Sara's old college. It was wonderful to talk to someone who knew her tutors and had worked in the Victorian splendour of the annexe on the hill. Sara ended up saying she had a bit of money to invest and might be interested in some of the paintings.

'Why don't you come round at seven one evening?' Jenny suggested. 'I'll provide the wine and some cheese, and we can have a really good natter and a look through all my stock.'

The encounter excited Sara. Suddenly she had something to do with her money that could bring

133

pleasure to herself and profit to others. She wanted to help Jenny make a go of her business. Her mind raced on: she might even offer to invest in it; become a partner even.

In the end she bought four paintings: two water-colours by Sven, an acrylic by an unknown called Moira Stephens and a striking portrait in oils by a young man called Jock whom Jenny assured her would make a name for himself one day. The bill came to just under seven thousand pounds and Sara had to stifle a snort when Jenny asked if she were sure she could afford it.

'I'm going to an auction on Friday,' Jenny told her as she left with the paintings. 'Would you like to come along?'

Sara went and thoroughly enjoyed herself, purchasing another three paintings. The house was starting to look different with all that modern art on the walls; she had an urge to redecorate, but she restrained herself. No point in doing that if the house had to go on the market, she told herself gloomily. So the paintings hung there, incongruously bright and clashing with the wallpaper.

Although she had more leave due to her, Sara decided that she ought to contact Jon Marsh, her boss. Her former boss, she corrected herself, since she'd decided that no way could she return to her old job. He would be disappointed, she knew that, but in retrospect her job had been mostly drudgery and she wasn't prepared to put up with it now that she didn't have to. She phoned the office and felt bad when he sounded so pleased to hear from her. Putting on her most businesslike voice, she arranged a meeting with him for the following morning.

Jon Marsh was looking harassed when she walked in, wearing a new pale-blue suit. 'That temp is hopeless.' He sighed, throwing his arms in the air. Then his face brightened as he saw her properly. 'Oh, you do look lovely. Always so smart. When are you coming back, Sara? I just can't manage without you.'

She took a deep breath. 'I'm afraid you're going to have to, Jon. I'm giving in my notice.'

'What? You can't do this to me. Why?'

She'd worked out her answer in advance. She was stressed out and wanted to rethink her life, perhaps go for something more artistic like she'd always wanted. Guy had recently been promoted, so they weren't short of cash, and she wanted to take her time over the job hunting, find something that was really right for her.

'I always knew you were too good for us,' Jon said ruefully. 'But at least let me offer you dinner tonight, as a token of my appreciation.'

Feeling somewhat starved of company, she agreed to meet him at the office at seven. She spent some time getting ready, carefully choosing a dress that was pretty without being too provocative and understating her make-up. She chose a light, floral scent and set out, arriving at the office just as Jon was stepping through the door. He looked very handsome in a casual blue shirt and navy jacket.

'The car's parked round the corner,' he said. 'Did you take a cab?'

'No, it was such a lovely evening I walked from the Tube.'

'You see how conveniently we're sited, Sara? Just five minutes' walk from two Underground stations. And I'm thinking of introducing limited flexitime. I think you should reconsider.'

Gently she pressed her fingers to his lips. 'Sh, Jon. If you're going to talk like that, I'm going straight home. Let's not talk business tonight, eh? Promise?'

He grinned at her. 'OK. Come on, then.'

Sara had always enjoyed his company and tonight was no exception. Now that he was no longer her boss, she felt free to treat him as the attractive male he undoubtedly was and, despite her vow not to get involved with him, her heart was skipping beats as he drove her in his smooth, sporty car through West London, following the line of the river. The last time she'd ridden in a car like this she was with Karl in Malibu, and look how that had turned out, she warned herself. But at a distance the memory was exhilarating rather than dampening.

They reached Barnes, where Jon lived. She'd never visited his flat and now she presumed he had chosen a restaurant local to him, one he knew well. So she was taken aback when he drew up outside a maisonette close to the river in a residential street.

'I thought I'd cook for you myself,' he smiled. 'My own version of Indonesian. You'll love it.'

'You never said . . .'

His eyes twinkled naughtily at her. 'I know, but would you have agreed to come into the lion's den if I had?'

She gave him an arch look. 'I'm not sure I'm agreeing, now.'

'Well it's up to you. But I've waited a long time to have you all to myself, just for one evening. If

136

you leave me in the lurch now, I shan't be a happy chappie. And I might just insist on you working out your full notice.'

'Hey, that's blackmail.'

'You should take it as a compliment. It shows how keen I am to show off my culinary prowess.'

'As long as it's only your *culinary* prowess.'

Sara was used to carrying on this type of banter with him, but now it seemed they were playing for higher stakes. As long as I don't drink too much, I can handle it, she told herself as she gave in and followed him to the steps leading up to his front door.

The flat was compact but very tastefully decorated in a mixture of Victorian and modern. Sara sank into a comfortable chair upholstered in a William Morris print – the familiar 'Blackthorn' design, scattered flowers and sinuous foliage on a dark-green background. There was a drawing of Barnes Bridge on the wall and some other London scenes opposite. Jon put some light jazz on and offered her a pre-prandial tipple.

'Do you have any fruit juice?' she asked.

His smile was wry. 'Don't worry, I'm not out to get you pissed.'

'I know, I'm just thirsty. Orange juice would do fine, with some ice if you have any.'

Jon was in and out of his small kitchen from then on, bringing her nibbles, changing the music, and carrying on an intermittent conversation that ranged from the price of property to food and drink. Sara felt at ease chatting with him, just as she used to in the office, but when he brought in the fragrant, steaming dishes he'd been preparing she knew that she was in for a real treat.

He turned out to be a superb cook. The chicken breast was succulent in its peanut sauce garnished with fresh coriander, and the stir-fried vegetables were a revelation, each cooked to perfection and glistening with colour.

'It's all down to the timing,' he told her. 'You have to know exactly when to add each item. Some veg need a lot longer than others. Some, like the mangetout, should only go in at the last minute.'

After home-made coconut ice-cream with a mango sorbet, Sara was in heaven. They'd drunk a light, spicy Gewürztraminer through the meal and her taste buds were still absorbing the wonderful blend of flavours. They went through to the sitting room and sipped Turkish coffee, then Jon brought out the brandy. It was extremely good Napoleon brandy.

'All right, just a snifter,' she agreed.

The music of some sexy female blues singer, the scent of the food still lingering in the air and the effect of the alcohol, all combined to make Sara feel cosy and relaxed, but suddenly the conversation took a turn which disconcerted her.

'I like it here, but I could do with a bigger place,' Jon was saying. 'There are some beautiful homes just down the road in Richmond, of course, but I can't see myself ever being able to afford to live there. Not unless I won the lottery. I forgot to check my ticket last week and someone said there were lots of fours, so I really convinced myself I'd won because there are some number fours in my entry. But would you believe it, when I checked, I found hardly any were the same.'

Sara heard herself say, as if from far away, 'Ah well, that's the luck of the draw, I suppose.'

'What would you do if you won the lottery, Sara?'

How tempted she was to tell him. It would be so simple just to blurt out, 'Actually, I have,' but the consequences might be disastrous. He would guess that was why she was leaving her job and berate her for not being honest with him.

'I . . . I'm not sure,' she stammered.

'You do play the lottery, I take it?'

'Sometimes.'

'You know, it's strange, nobody seems to think of the consequences of winning when they put down their numbers each week. I mean, what could you or I do with a couple of million? Apart from what almost everybody thinks of – new house, new car, world cruise, treat the family . . . Same old boring stuff. But you could set up a business, do something you've always wanted to do. Me, I'd buy shares in a racehorse or a stud farm. How about you?'

'I suppose I'd set up an art gallery, or something. There's a new one that's just opened near me.'

After that, the pressure was off as the conversation turned to art. Sara was so relieved that when he sat on the arm of her chair to show her a book of Picasso's erotic prints she leant against him and allowed him to put his arm around her shoulder. Soon he was stroking her hair, evidently aroused by the cavorting figures portrayed in rampant poses in sections, titled *The Brothel*, *The Voyeur* and *The Orgy*. The gravures reminded her of Indian erotic art.

'It's making me feel quite horny, looking at those,' Jon said, his voice husky.

'That's the whole idea, isn't it?' Sara turned

around with a grin but her smile froze. The look on Jon's face made it plain that he was feeling very randy indeed; before she could shut the book and move away, his mouth swooped down onto hers like a marauding hawk and engaged her in a passionate kiss.

At first she scrabbled helplessly at his arms, trying to shake him off, but as the irresistible energy of his desire flooded through her she felt herself weakening, wanting it. In her head the voice of protest was feeble while a stronger voice asked: Why not? It would be a nice way to say goodbye after the two years she had worked for him, a kind of friendly conclusion to their relationship, now that he was no longer her boss and she was no longer kidding herself that Guy gave a damn about who she slept with.

Sara sighed as his hands crept to unbutton her prim dress, exposing her cleavage in the white lace bra. His fingers moved delicately around her throat and her shoulders, while his lips softened their impact, growing lush and sensual, now that he was sure she wasn't going to wriggle away. She tasted the fruitiness of his tongue, traces of mango and coconut still lingering, and smelt the spicy lavender of his aftershave – *Fahrenheit*, she thought it was. Her body yielded in his embrace, softening against him as he slipped into the chair and raised her onto his lap so that he could explore her more thoroughly.

'This is heaven,' she heard him murmur. 'If you only knew how many times I've dreamed of you.'

She gave a soft chuckle, low in her throat, and began to caress him back. Her hands traced the smooth contours of his cheeks, feeling the slight

140

roughness below the surface, and ran lightly over his Adam's apple to the hollow in his throat. She wanted him, there was no question about that. Perhaps she always had, only she'd been too scared of losing both her job and her marriage to respond to his advances. Well, none of that mattered any more.

Now he had the whole of her front unbuttoned and was delving into the stiff cups of her bra, his fingers fumbling around her nipples. Sara wanted more direct contact and felt behind her back to release the fastening, giving her breasts free rein. Jon goggled when he saw them, his hands cupping them reverently as he said, 'Oh, they're even lovelier than I'd imagined,' and they swelled with pride.

His mouth bent to kiss each of them in turn, moving slowly up their steep sides towards the firm nipples. While he manipulated them with his tongue, sending Sara into wild spirals of delight, his hands stroked the bare patch of skin on her inner thighs, between her stocking-tops and her panties. She could feel her pussy turning to cream within the cotton of her panties and wondered how long it would take before he got in there. He was hot for her now, barely restraining himself, and she knew if she gave him the least encouragement he'd be diving in like a shot.

Tentatively she reached down and felt the solid ridge beneath his fly, running her thumb and forefinger down either side of its length to gauge its size. He groaned into her ear and, when she took her hand away, replaced it immediately. Sara grew reckless, squeezing his cock through his trousers with no regard for his hair-trigger arousal. It pleased her that he wanted her so much. Thinking about all those sultry summer days at the office when she'd worn skimpy tops and miniskirts, knowing she was impossibly tempting to him, was a real turn-on. On one occasion he had come out of the toilets looking very red in the face and she was sure he'd been jerking off in there, thinking about her.

Jon made an inarticulate noise in his throat as she found his zip and began to pull it down. His erection felt huge inside his pants, and as she pulled the glans free of the waistband he gave a loud groan and his cock pushed up into her hand like a pet craving attention. She stroked the end with her thumb then pulled his pants down to reveal the rest of the shaft. Thick and strong, it jerked so violently when it was released that she was afraid he would come there and then.

But then he calmed down, and Sara stroked his cock between her two palms.

'That feels fantastic,' Jon murmured. 'Please, can we get onto the carpet? It will be easier lying down.'

It was soon obvious what he had in mind. He wanted them to get into the sixty-nine position and Sara willingly obliged, tearing off her white panties so that he could reach her pussy with his lips. She wasn't quite so happy about sucking him. Although she liked to lick up and down the shaft and across the ball of his glans she had a horror of having him, or any man, come in her mouth, since she hated the taste of spunk. It had been a source of contention between her and Guy until he'd learnt to accept that she was entitled to her sexual likes and dislikes just as much as he was. Now, she

142

hoped that Jon wouldn't try to force his cock down her throat.

Still, it was pleasurable to taste the solidness of him, to feel his cock swell and throb beneath her lips and tongue. When he began to lick her, probing between the fat petals of her labia to find the tender bud within, Sara relaxed into it with a sigh and opened her legs wide, feeling his soft hair tickle her thighs as he went at it with renewed enthusiasm. Jon was a good licker, applying just the right degree of force to her clitoris and knowing when to stimulate the other parts of her pussy as well.

Soon he was playing at finger-fucking her, driving her to the edge of frustration as he dabbled in her entrance and made her juices run. Just when she felt she could bear no more of his titillation he plunged his forefinger right inside, feeling the cushioned velvet of her quim close around his finger with crushing force in her eagerness to wrest every nuance of pleasure from his penetration. After that he withdrew for a while, leaving her achingly empty inside while he concentrated his efforts around her breasts and clitoris again, sucking at her nipples while he fingered her rapidly down below. Sara felt the seesaw swing of her arousal kick in, her attention divided three ways between her tingling nipples, her throbbing clitoris and her needy, desperate quim.

He was a clit-teaser, she decided, perhaps in revenge for all those occasions when she would flirt with him in the office but then turn down his request for a date. He obviously thought of her as a prick-teaser too. Well, she'd show him how it should be done! Her tongue lapped at his glans with delicate precision, making him thrust upwards. But she was always ready for him and made sure he didn't gain access to her mouth. She kept him hovering on the brink in the same way that he teased her, licking and sucking him lightly but never allowing him to enter the warm cave of her mouth and spurt into her throat as he was obviously longing to do.

Their encounter took on all the hallmarks of a sparring match as each of them grew more frenetic in their quest for satisfaction. When Jon made one of his occasional forays into her vagina Sara contracted her muscles around his finger and held it tight, as if she'd never let him go. And when she slipped up and his cock found its way momentarily between her lips he would push boldly home, forcing her to seize his cock by the root and hold it still while she extricated it from her mouth. They continued like this for some time, each one see-sawing between encouragement and denial.

It was a strange love–hate relationship, not unlike that of boss and employee. Sara began to view it as a race; whoever reached orgasm first would win. She wanted to come so badly, yet whenever she was near Jon would back off and leave her high and dry. Her only satisfaction was in doing the same to him. It was a weird form of power-play and she wished that she'd never started, but now she was committed to coming out on top, and that meant gaining her satisfaction before he got his.

Somehow she sensed that Jon knew the rules too. He had an uncanny knack of knowing just when to pull out of her, or to stop licking. His approach was incredibly arousing, so she knew that if ever she did reach her goal the resulting climax would be extremely intense. But she knew that her satisfaction would be incomplete unless she also cheated him of his. Grimly determined, she began to focus on the kind of images that usually brought her off, but it was hard to concentrate.

Then she thought of Guy and everything suddenly clicked into place. It wasn't really Jon she wanted power over, after all; it was her husband. He'd made her feel impotent, useless, and she could never forgive him for that. Jon was suffering her misplaced revenge, that was all. Once she realised that, it was easy. In her imagination it was Guy's prick that she was teasing, Guy's orgasm she was trying to forestall. She began to move her hips and pelvis in an aggressive, circular motion, thrusting her pubic mound against his face so that she gained greater stimulation, and soon she felt the inevitable ascent towards ecstasy begin.

The climax was all she'd expected and more, spasms of pure bliss that seemed to repeat in an endless loop of sensation. She felt the strong, muscular sensuality of them rack through her again and again, making her belly shudder and her breasts grow hot and huge, turning her whole body into a vehicle of erotic pleasure that carried her on and on in ever-increasing ecstasy until the thrills began to subside and slow down, becoming little aftershocks instead of a huge explosion, quietening down at last into gentle ripples.

Sara had forgotten all about Jon and his importunate erection. It lay there, still at half-mast, while she sat up and pulled on her pants. He was looking at her through glazed eyes, still in some half-dream. 'What is it, Sara?' he asked, his tone slightly anxious, as he saw her fasten her bra again. 'What are you doing?'

She scrambled to her feet and pulled on her dress, thrust her feet into her shoes. 'Thanks, Jon, for the lovely meal and everything.'

'What?' He sat up, his eyes red and unattractive, his hair a mess. 'You're not leaving, are you? Not yet.'

'I'm afraid I must.'

She was already moving towards the door. He was Guy, remember? It was unfair, she knew that, to punish one man for the sins of another, but then again, when had anyone claimed that life was fair? With the spirit of feminism rampant in her heart, she ignored the voice of protest that was feebly throbbing in her rear and went through the door into the night. Hurrying off in a reckless mood, she made towards Richmond Tube station, hoping that the last train hadn't gone.

Luckily it hadn't. As Sara sped on her way back home, a few pangs of remorse assailed her, but she couldn't go back. Perhaps she would send him flowers, she thought with a smile. It made a change to be acting like a male chauvinist, loving and leaving him in the lurch. She could picture him now, frantically jerking off where she had left him lying on the floor. That would teach him to sexually harass his employees.

But her feeling of triumph was short-lived when she remembered that Guy was due home in a couple of days. What kind of prospects did their marriage have now?

Even so, as she waited for Guy's call from the airport to say that he was on his way home, Sara

146

felt vaguely hopeful that things would work out for them. She had made an effort to get the house clean and tidy. The fridge was full of his favourite beer and snacks, in case he felt hungry. There were clean sheets on the bed. She had showered, washed her hair and put on his favourite dress. I will make an effort, she told herself. With luck, Malibu might just turn out to be a passing fantasy.

But the instant Guy walked in through the door and looked around his face twisted into a frown. 'What the hell's all that?' were his first words.

For a few seconds Sara had no idea what he meant. Then light dawned. 'Oh, you mean the paintings? There's this new gallery opened in Hawker's Lane and I thought I'd buy some pictures . . .'

Her voice tailed away as he snapped, 'Take them down. They don't go with the wallpaper.'

He could not have stunned her more if he'd thrown a bucket of pigswill over her. Within seconds, Sara was angrier than she'd been for a long time. She was about to berate him when the phone rang and he went to answer it, striding across the room before she could get there.

'Oh, Mum! How are you?'

Sara stalked from the room, her anger curdling in her veins. This was some homecoming! She sat in the kitchen while she waited for the kettle to boil hoping that she could manage to simmer down. After she'd drunk two cups of extra-strong coffee Guy entered the room.

'That was Mum. Why didn't you ring and tell her I was on a business trip or something?'

'Why should I? She's your mother.'

'But you know we didn't want her to get

147

suspicious about our win. I had to invent some-thing on the spur of the moment. I told her you'd kicked me out.'

'What?'

'I said we were having marital difficulties. After all, that's not far from the truth, is it?' He sneered. 'I told her we were in the process of talking things through. She said she'd like to see me soon, so I invited her over.'

'You did what?'

'Be reasonable, Sara.'

'No, you be reasonable! You've not been back five minutes and you're doing your best to upset me in every way you can think of. Well sod you, Guy Kingsley!'

She stormed out, unsure where to go or what to do. There was a flood of tears dammed up inside her and she wanted to let it out, but she was damned if she would give Guy the satisfaction of seeing her cry. Pulling on her jacket, she took the car keys out of her bag and went out, slamming the front door behind her.

Sara drove for ages through the London streets until she came to a park. It was almost empty at that time of day and she sat down on a bench and put her head in her hands. The cruel shock of Guy's homecoming had reduced her to a bewil-dered mess and she had to try and sort herself out before facing her husband again.

Chapter Nine

TRY AS SHE might, Sara couldn't help getting
embroiled in Guy's family squabbles. It irked her
that both Mark and Penny tried to get her to take
sides against the other, each claiming that they
were squandering the money they'd been given.
There were heavy hints from both sides, too, that
they deserved a bit more. Sara found it sickening
and she told Guy so.

'It's not really any of your business, it it?' he
said, coldly.

'Then tell your brother and sister that. See if you
can get them to stop ringing me up and going on
about each other.'

She made sure that she was out visiting a friend
when Guy's mother came round. Sara had always
found Anne Kingsley a difficult woman, who
considered her not good enough for her elder son.
It was doubtful whether she would approve of any
woman he chose. Now, with their marriage going
through a tricky patch and the news of their win
being kept secret, Sara wanted to have even less to
do with her.

Wanting to become more involved in the art
scene again, Sara began visiting galleries and

spending more time with Emily. One day she was talking about how much she'd enjoyed art school when Emily said, 'Why don't you try your hand at painting yourself, instead of just looking at other people's work? I'd be interested to see what you can do.'

'Not very much now, I suppose,' Sara said ruefully.

'But you've got it all there somewhere, surely? And you have the time, now you've stopped work. Why not pop into Mag's shop and buy some paints? I'm sure you won't regret it.'

Sara said that she might do just that but promptly forgot all about it. Even so, the next time she passed the art shop and saw the display of artists' materials in the window she went in. Ten minutes later she emerged with two bags full of watercolours, brushes, sketchbooks, a palette and some sizing. She didn't feel up to oils yet but the prospect of doing some watercolour sketches was very appealing. Landscapes had always been her forte and now she couldn't wait to get in the car and drive somewhere scenic.

Sara told Guy she was going out for the day on Saturday, taking a picnic and doing some sketching, maybe some painting too. She'd hoped he might show some interest but he seemed indifferent to her renewed enthusiasm for art. She left on Saturday morning with a heavy heart, but when the day brightened and the streets of London gave way to the fields of Surrey she began to feel happier. It was wonderful to be going back to a pleasure long neglected, to be doing something creative again.

Just as she got out of the car at Box Hill,

however, the heavens opened with a deluge and a steady downpour set in. She made a couple of sketches from the car but it was obvious that her outdoor painting would have to be postponed. Disappointed, she toyed with the idea of exploring the area, but the rain was so heavy and lending such an unpleasant chill to the air that she turned back towards London and drove straight home.

The house was so quiet that she thought Guy must be out, but his raincoat was hanging in the hall along with his umbrella, and it was still bucketing down. Puzzled, she looked all around downstairs and then wondered if he'd gone up to lie down. She went upstairs and heard faint, unusual sounds coming from their bedroom. Was the television on in there? Some instinct made her tiptoe to the door and open it very slowly and quietly.

Sara's fears were confirmed the instant she peeped through the crack into the darkened room. By the light of a bedside lamp, draped with a pink cloth to give a subdued glow, she could see Guy and a strange woman performing some equally strange ritual. Evidently her husband hadn't expected her to return this soon. He was naked, except for a black silk blindfold and a pair of black leather gauntlets that were strapped together, effectively handcuffing him. She was struck by the sensual shape of his mouth as he knelt on the bed, his lips forming a perfect soft pout. It was impossible to ignore the sight of his erection too, rising fierce and proud from between his thighs.

The woman wore only a black leather corset, cut low over the breasts and high over the buttocks, with fishnet stockings and black patent shoes with high stiletto heels. Her long black hair fell loose about her shoulders and she had an impressive figure. When she turned round, Sara saw that she had a classically beautiful face, too, although the red lips were curved in a sneer and her dark eyes were hard and humourless. Black net fingerless gloves reached to her elbow and Sara gasped when she saw the woman holding a short-handled whip.

The sound was tiny, but enough to alert the woman, who turned towards the door with a start. She ducked away, but not soon enough. The woman came striding to the door and pulled it open, but instead of looking shocked her red lips opened in a wide grin and she beckoned her into the room. Sara followed, spellbound, watching the dominatrix wield her lash like an expert. It snaked out and caught Guy unawares on the arm. He winced with sudden pain, but afterwards a look of bliss stole over his face.

Fascinated, Sara watched the woman walk around the bed. She gave Guy a shove on the back and he fell forward onto all fours, his backside nakedly exposed. The dominatrix looked thoughtful as she moved this way and that, sizing up the task and considering alternatives. She smoothed a caressing hand over his left buttock as if testing the quality of his flesh. Sara felt absurdly excited at the way the silent drama was unfolding before her eyes, with no attempt by the strange woman at explanations or excuses. She was behaving as if she had a perfect right to be there – which, in a way, she had.

With a deft flick of the wrist, the black leather thong dealt Guy a stinging kiss on the meaty underside of his buttocks. He gave a low groan and his cock jerked angrily. The woman threw Sara a smile of complicity and raised one thin, black brow, offering her the handle of the whip. She drew back, horrified, but the woman just shrugged and paced around to the other side of the bed, sizing up the target again. This time the whip lashed Guy's other buttock but he was braced against it and the crack was louder, more satisfying as it caught the taut curve.

Sara felt her cheeks grow hot and her pulse ragged. She felt herself being drawn into the action by the stagy confidence of the dark-haired dominatrix. There was an inevitability about the encounter that some part of her recognised, turning her into an accomplice after the fact. It felt like the strange woman was her alter ego, punishing Guy for what he had done to their marriage, treating him as she secretly longed to treat him herself. Even though she couldn't quite bring herself to use that serious-looking whip on him with her own hands, Sara approved of the chastisement that was being meted out to him. Approved and enjoyed the sight of him blindly flinching and suffering, wriggling like a worm on a hook.

She didn't care who this other woman was, whether some professional hired by phone or his personal mistress who knew his tastes. Right now she seemed like Sara's agent, her friend. The fact that Guy had no idea she was there, witnessing his humiliation, lent a satisfying excitement to the situation. She sank down onto the carpet by the door and settled with her back against the wall, waiting to see what would happen next.

The woman began talking to him in a low, intense voice that made the hairs on Sara's neck prickle. 'You are disgusting,' she heard. 'Look how

153

your miserable prick is enjoying itself. It won't be taught a lesson, will it? It just won't learn. So we'll have to find some other way to punish it.'

She found something in her bag that was standing open on the floor and approached the bed. Sara saw that it was a plug of black leather. The woman pushed his buttocks open with her thumb and forefinger, holding them apart while she inserted the anal plug. Guy groaned with pain as his arse was summarily invaded and left stoppered. His penis drooped a little, less sure of itself, and the woman gave a brief smile of pleasure, her eyes flicking momentarily towards Sara then back on target.

As the scenario proceeded Sara felt oddly detached. This couldn't be the man she had married, the man she'd won the lottery with. He had become alien, dehumanised almost, an object of derision. Something inside her snapped when she thought about how he had been towards her, how things had gone downhill since their win even though she had tried her best to breathe life into their failing marriage.

He'd told her he wanted freedom, the freedom to have other women and to experience perverse satisfaction, and he'd scarcely been able to wait until she was out of the house before grabbing whatever he could. But something final was happening: the last judgement had been served on him and now the sentence was being carried out with Sara's tacit approval.

'You are scum!' the woman was growling, the perfect voice of Sara's own anger and frustration. 'Not worthy to lick my shoes. But I will graciously allow you to lick them, miscreant. Put out your miserable tongue.'

Guy looked so ridiculous, kneeling with his plugged bum in the air, his eyes blindfolded and his long pink tongue hanging out, that Sara could scarcely stifle her laughter. The dominatrix remained deadly serious, however, as she thrust her pointed toe in his face and gave the curt command, 'Lick!'

Dog-like, he obeyed, the flat of his tongue wiping all over the shiny black leather toe. Then the spiky heel was thrust into his mouth for him to suck, like a black dildo. Whenever he failed to perform to the woman's satisfaction, the whip snaked over his head and caught him full on the curve of his buttock, eliciting a choking moan. Sara was growing more and more excited, wishing now that she hadn't refused to take part. It was hard to remain aloof when every cell in her body was crying out for revenge for what he had done to her, this very scene proof positive of his betrayal.

'Now you are warmed up, I want you to lick and suck something else,' she heard the woman say. 'And if you don't do it to my complete satisfaction, you'll know the taste of my whip again. Do you hear?'

He nodded vigorously. Then, to Sara's surprise, the woman turned and came towards her. She whispered in her ear, 'Want to take part?' Sara found herself nodding, hardly able to contain her excitement. The woman smelt of cheap scent and something indefinable. She added briskly, 'Take your knickers off.'

Sara did as she was told, her clitoris throbbing hungrily as she realised what she was letting herself in for. Through gesturing and grimacing the woman indicated what she wanted Sara to do, making her kneel before Guy on the bed and put her mons close to his face while she stood behind Sara to make sure her voice came from roughly the right direction.

'All right,' she said loudly, when Sara was in position. 'Now lick and suck my pussy until I come. Do it properly, or it will be the worse for you. Begin.'

Sara held her labia apart so that Guy's probing tongue could get to the intimate heart of her. She'd been rather disappointed by his cunnilingus in the past, it being usually a perfunctory act whose sole purpose was to get her wet enough for penetration. The idea that he would now be forced to continue until she was thoroughly satiated was a turn-on in itself. She could feel the swollen nub of her clitoris sticking out from its niche with bold assurance and, when the tip of his wet tongue found it, a shock of pure, electric pleasure coursed through her veins, triggering the upward spiral towards orgasm.

Guy began to lick her with enthusiasm, rolling his tongue around the convoluted folds of her vulva until he found the protuberant flesh he was seeking. His tonguing then became more focused, working her rhythmically until pulses of ecstasy were throbbing through her system, making her feel faint with desire. She swayed slightly and the woman caught her shoulders, holding her steady. Then, as Guy's actions intensified, Sara felt the faceless woman's hands creep to her breasts, stroking them through her T-shirt until her nipples felt huge and stiff.

Lost in her sensual heaven, Sara didn't give a damn that it was another woman's hands on her breasts, and soon she felt soft lips nuzzling at her neck and ears, too. She tilted back her head, half-overcome with bliss, and waited for the climactic moment to arrive. It didn't take long. As she ground her mons into Guy's blindfolded face and felt his tongue probe into her, his lips pressing hard against her outer labia, the first thrilling fore-taste of her climax had her groaning and swaying against the supportive body behind her.

'That's right, suck me off,' the woman said to Guy. Her commanding tone had the instant effect of making Guy redouble his efforts. Her words were also accompanied by fierce squeezing of Sara's breasts, and the combination of stimuli was enough to trigger the long-awaited orgasm. Sara collapsed with a low moan as she felt the tremulous spasms grow stronger and more gratifying, making her shudder voluptuously until they finally faded.

She was summarily lifted backwards off the bed by powerful arms and set back on her feet. Dazed and bewildered she looked into the cold, dark eyes of the dominatrix, who murmured, 'Now go, quick, before I take off the blindfold.'

Sara did as she was told; the woman wasn't the kind you argued with. As she left the bedroom, she could hear the woman barking more commands. She went into the bathroom and washed herself quickly, wondering what the hell to do next. Should she leave and return later, pretending noth-ing had happened? Should she lie low in the house?

Slowly it dawned on her that, not only did she not wish to stay in the house, she didn't want to see Guy again – ever again, if it could be avoided. Despite her delight at having got one over on him, and the warm thrill of sexual satisfaction that was all the sweeter for having been obtained under false pretences, Sara found that she despised her husband. She'd been prepared to make a go of things but he'd had no such intention, and enough was enough.

Pausing only to grab her purse containing her renewed gold card, Sara picked up her raincoat and umbrella from the hall stand and went through the front door, closing it quietly behind her. Now she understood what Guy had meant when he'd talked about freedom. She had never felt more free in her life. She could go anywhere she liked, do anything she pleased. Getting into the car she drove down the street the same way she had a thousand times before, only this time she was truly in control.

Driving through the late Saturday afternoon streets, seeing people struggling home with their shopping, Sara began to think about getting away from it all. Her short-lived excusion into the country had made her long for green fields and wooded hills. Suddenly, a vision of Ireland came into her mind. She'd had a wonderful holiday in County Kerry when she was a teenager, staying in a caravan belonging to a friend's family, and she'd always promised herself that she would return some day. What better time than the present?

It was half past four and there was a travel agent still open. Sara hurried in and was soon discussing her plan breathlessly with an assistant. There were no flights available for a week or so, she was told, but she could go by ferry tomorrow if she wished. Once in Ireland she could hire a cottage, which would be no problem at this time of year. It was all music to Sara's ears. She decided to buy whatever clothes and toiletries she needed then drive to Wales, where she would spend the night in Holyhead and take the ferry across next day.

Ireland was even lovelier than she'd remembered: green and soft like new-grown leaves, with a clarity to the air that was both refreshing and gentle. Even the rain felt as pure and caressing to her cheek as baby kisses. She drove until it began to get dark and stopped at the first B&B sign she saw, in a litle village called Kilmoran. She was the only guest, and Mrs Murphy fussed over her like a mother hen until Sara retreated into her attic room with a cup of tea and sat looking out of the window at the clear stars and brooding about her future.

She needed a rest, a good long rest, to revive her spirits and heal her wounds. Fortunately her paints and brushes had still been in the car so she had something to be going on with. The prospect of painting all this beautiful scenery was very inspiring and she could hardly wait to get started. But staying in guest houses was not what she wanted to do. It was fine for the first night, but she needed to be independent. She would find some remote cottage to rent.

Next morning Sara travelled towards the west coast, trying to remember where she had stayed all those years ago. She wanted to feel like a teenager again, starting out in life instead of picking up the pieces. Suddenly the road signs became familiar and it all came flooding back: the lake where they had fished, the mountain they had climbed, the twisty lane leading to the forge where the blacksmith still plied his sweaty trade. Even the village shop where they had bought ice-cream on a hot day was still standing, complete with the old-fashioned soft drinks advertisement nailed to the bulging stone wall. She went into the shop-cum-post office and inquired about cottages for rent.

'Oh, you'll be wanting Paddy McGuire's place; down the road and turn left. You can't miss it – unless you go the wrong way,' said the bespectacled postmistress, with impeccable Irish logic. 'If you'll wait ten minutes, I'll get my Sean to go with you. Would you like a cup of tea while you're waiting?'

Sara agreed to wait and eventually Sean appeared, a gangly teenager with a winsome smile. He wouldn't get in the car but set out ahead with a stick in his hand which he wielded like a weapon against the straggling cow parsley, whistling like a virtuoso all the while. He led her to a tumbledown farmhouse and insisted on going up and banging on the door for her, making sure that there was someone at home and they weren't all out in the fields. When Paddy's wife appeared he took his leave, refusing to take the pound coin she tried to press into his palm.

'He's a good lad, that Sean,' Mrs McGuire said, approvingly. 'Now, what was it you wanted, m'dear?'

There were holiday cottages to let on the McGuires' land at a ridiculously low rent. Over another cup of tea Sara made a provisional agreement to take one for a month.

'You can have your pick, now we're out of season,' Mrs McGuire smiled. 'What made you take a holiday in October, may I ask?'

'Oh, I wanted to do some painting and I thought it would be quieter now.'

'Painting? You're an artist, are you? How wonderful.'

'I'm not much of one. If I get fed up with my own company, is there a pub in the village? I didn't see one as I came through.'

'You'll be better off going into Ballylee,' she was told. 'It's nearer to where the cottages are, and the drink's better too, so my husband tells me. They always have a bit of a ceilidh in the barn at the back there on a Saturday night.'

They drove to the three cottages, once inhabited by farm hands and their families, which had been done up in a simple but practical fashion, with whitewashed walls hung with local photographs, Irish linen curtains and bedspreads, and rush matting on the stone floors. There was a kitchen diner, a bedroom and a small bathroom. It was very basic, but exactly what Sara felt she needed to restore her sense of proportion.

'I'll take this one,' she smiled.

Mrs McGuire's blue eyes rounded in surprise. 'Don't you want to see the other two, before you make your choice?'

'No, this is fine. I have a lovely view of the hills and if it gets chilly I can light the fire. I'll be fine.'

'Well if you're sure, I'll send my eldest over with some milk and butter and bread, and some fresh eggs for the morning. I'll put the electric blanket on now to make sure the bed is aired. There's tea and other things in the kitchen cabinet, but if you want anything just knock at the door.'

'Thank you, Mrs McGuire. You're very kind.'

Sara longed to be alone. She handed the Irishwoman twenty pounds on account, a crisp note straight from the cash dispenser, and was glad when the woman finally stopped fussing and left her to enjoy the peace and quiet. Half an hour later, while she was running a bath by courtesy of a fierce-sounding Ascot heater, a shy boy knocked at the door with a wicker basket, its contents covered by a check teacloth. She felt as if she had slipped back into another era.

If they knew I was a millionaire, they'd think I was mad to be staying here, Sara thought with wry satisfaction. But it was what she needed. She had never been more sure of anything in her life.

For five days Sara lived like a hermit, going out into the beautiful countryside to sketch and paint when the weather permitted, or staying in and putting the finishing touches to her work when it was wet. Mrs McGuire's eldest son called each morning to deposit fresh milk on her doorstep and sometimes other things, too: some goat's cheese, apples or a pot of home-made jam. The feeling that she had slipped back several decades deepened as the days went by and her solitude brought with it the first true relaxation she'd experienced for years. Even thoughts of Guy began to fade, and the lottery win began to seem like a fairy-tale fantasy that had happened to someone else. Only this was real, this secluded heaven surrounded by gently rolling hills with the dips between offering a distant glimpse of the wild Atlantic.

On Saturday morning she accepted Paddy McGuire's offer of a lift into the nearest small town and she went on a minor shopping spree in the old-fashioned department store, using her gold card to buy some more clothes and a stout pair of walking shoes. The shop assistant looked at her askance and consulted the manager. Evidently gold cards were few and far between in that part of the world. But when all was found to be in order she was given her purchases beautifully wrapped in a brown paper parcel tied up with string, the way she remembered from her childhood.

She was invited to lunch with the McGuires but declined the offer, wanting solitude again. But by the late afternoon, Sara was craving company. She remembered that there would be a ceilidh at the local inn that night, and decided to go along. The hospitality of the Irish was legendary after all, so she was sure that she'd be made welcome. Dressing in her newly acquired skirt of green Irish linen, teamed with a white, lace-trimmed blouse, and with silver buckles on her low-heeled shoes, she thought she looked the part.

As she walked down the country lane in the twilight Sara could hear the sound of a fiddle and the drumming beat of a bodhrán. Her pace quickened as she saw the lights in the old barn behind the Dog and Whistle. Cars were being parked at the front of the pub and there was a general air of bustle that made her heart race. This was going to be something special.

The atmosphere in the old barn was warm and friendly, with everyone sitting on crude benches around an open space and the musicians in a gallery that had been the hay-loft. When the mournful strains of the uillean pipes rang out everyone fell silent in respect, and tears came into Sara's eyes as the piper played his beautiful melody. The notes faded away, and then a man stood up to sing.

He was tall and dark, with glossy hair reaching in a tousled mass to his shoulders, and his eyes were bright green. He stood erect, his slim figure emphasised by the open-necked white shirt and tight-fitting black trousers. Round his slender waist was a black leather belt with a snake's head clasp and he wore little green leather boots, reminding her of a leprechaun. Sara was fascinated by the way he looked and he soon had her in thrall with his rich, deep voice, singing in Gaelic of some enduring sorrow. When his eyes were not closed in concentration they looked straight at her, piercing her soul with their bright intensity.

His song ended and the musicians provided him with a lilting rhythm. His feet began to move of their own accord and still he was staring at her, upright and proud as if challenging her – the English woman, the stranger – to step into his foreign, Celtic world. Sara sat there rapt, scarcely aware that several others were creeping onto the dance floor to join him, the tapping rhythm of heels and toes swelling the musicians' beat.

The middle-aged woman beside her stood up, jerking Sara back into sudden realisation that almost everyone else was dancing. The woman smiled and took her hand. 'Come and try it,' she said. 'I'll show you the basic step. It's easy; anyone can do it.'

Cautiously Sara followed her onto the floor and soon got the hang of the tapping heel–toe rhythm. There was something hypnotic and exhilarating about it, she discovered, and soon her feet were moving automatically, allowing her eyes to rove around the room and find the handsome soloist once more. He was there in the thick of it and, when she caught his eye, he smiled at her. She blushed and looked away, unable to hold such a frank and sexy gaze. He stood out in the company, the most virile and handsome man in the room – and most probably the village lecher, as well. He was a man to steer clear of, that was for sure.

Dancing as if her life depended on it, Sara succeeded in wearing herself out and working up a terrible thirst. Eventually, she had to rush to the bar to order a pint of lemonade. While she was gulping it down, Mr McGuire came up.

'It's good to see you enjoying yourself,' he smiled. 'I was beginning to worry about you, all alone in the cottage. It's not healthy for a fine young woman like yourself, I was thinking. But now here you are, dancing along with the rest of us. And what do you think of our Saturday socials? Nothing like it in England, I suppose.'

'Not that *I've* ever known.' She smiled back. 'It beats the disco scene any day, as far as I'm concerned. The musicians play so marvellously, and that singer . . .' She faltered, afraid to show too much interest in the man, but Paddy picked up the cue at once.

'Ah, that's our Liam. He's a fine performer, is Liam O'Connor.' His dark eyes twinkled at her, as if he knew that any woman must be smitten the instant she laid eyes on such a fine performer.

'What does he do?' she couldn't resist asking.

'He's a scholar, a collector of Irish lore and music. When he's not here in his native village, he's working in Dublin, at the university there. You see, he has a fine brain too. A paragon of all virtue is our Liam.'

There was an irony in his tone that was not lost on Sara. She took it as a tacit warning not to get too involved nor inquire too closely about him. But the air of mystery surrounding the man only served to make her more curious about him. When she went back into the barn her eyes darted around eagerly but he had vanished and the woman who had led her into the dance came up to make conversation. She was obviously curious about what this young Englishwoman was doing in their midst, but she seemed to accept Sara's explanation that she had come there to paint.

'Sure, the scenery around here is the best you'll find anywhere in the world,' the woman said, her face shining with pleasure.

The crowd was dispersing into the night. Sara looked out and found that it was pitch-black beyond the cosy yellow light thrown by the inn and barn, so when Mr McGuire offered to squire her home she accepted gratefully. As they were walking along the lane, a man passed on his bicycle, giving a ring on his bell and a cheery wave. With a shock, Sara realised that it was Liam O'Connor. She was glad it was dark, to hide her blushes, and was relieved when he went on cycling into the night with brisk energy.

The romantic Irishman wasn't finished with her yet, however. When she lay tucked up in the old-fashioned brass bedstead covered with a hand-made quilt, his handsome face returned to haunt her. She knew that it was dangerous to think too much about him. A man like that must have at least one woman, and a host of others waiting hopefully in the wings. Her conscious mind was able to censor her lustful thoughts, but once she was asleep and dreaming there was no stopping her imagination . . . .

She was alone in the hills, the wonderful hills

that she'd been trying to capture in paint all week, and there was the sound of hoof beats, as loud and insistent as that of the bodhrán. A white horse came galloping over a high hill as if it had come straight from the ocean, its mane flying and its eyes wide. Riding it bareback was a Celtic warrior, his dark mane flying as free as the horse's pale one, and his eyes were burning like emeralds beneath his straight black brows.

Seeing her alone, the knight slowed and put out his arm as he rode towards her. With one giant sweep he caught Sara round the waist and pulled her up in front of him, kicking his heels into the horse's sweaty flanks to pick up speed again. Breathlessly she felt the sandals fall from her feet as the gallop resumed, and she gripped handfuls of the horse's hairy mane to keep her steady, although there was no need with the man's protective arm around her. He held her close to his warm body and she could feel her breasts pressing against his forearm while his strong thighs kept her in place.

He was murmuring to her in Gaelic, soft seductive phrases that both mystified and excited her. She knew that he had come to claim her as his own, and she also knew that she would not resist. The allure of his powerful masculinity was too strong, too compelling. She felt weak as water in his presence, her body recognising the masterful force that required her to yield or else forfeit her one chance of happiness in this life.

On and on they raced over the dark hills until day dawned and he took her into a walled garden filled with the scent of flowers, the songs of birds and the humming of insects. He lay her down tenderly on the daisy-strewn grass and took off his belt with its giant sword. Once disarmed, he lay down beside her and claimed her with a single, overpowering kiss. Sara felt her senses reel as his soft mouth grew more greedy, more demanding, and her body melted into his.

Soon she felt as if she were floating six inches off the ground, her body as insubstantial as air. The kiss infused her being with joy and light, so that by the time he stripped off her clothes she felt already naked. Her breasts were straining to receive his lips, the nipples hot and stiff and yearning. Her quim was streaming with honeyed juices, begging him silently to drink. And her womb was trembling for him, craving a partner for the weaving dance of bliss . . . .

It was from this state of extreme arousal that Sara awoke, just before the dawn. She was shivering and found that, caught in the throes of her erotic dream, she had kicked all the bedclothes onto the floor. The Celtic warrior's face – Liam O'Connor's face – was still haunting her. The warmth of those strong arms was still enfolding her, and she felt bereft. A deep sadness seized her, born of frustrated longing, and she got up to make herself a comforting cup of tea.

While she drank it, watching the sun rise behind the hills, Sara knew beyond all doubt that her marriage to Guy was over. She needed to feel that rapturous love again, that optimism, that sense of being fully, vitally alive. And she promised herself that she wouldn't stop seeking it; nor, when she found it, would she let it go.

Chapter Ten

ON MONDAY MORNING Sara decided to walk into the village to get more provisions. She set out down the winding lane and was soon in a world of her own, humming softly to herself as she ambled beside bunches of faded cow parsley, accompanied by the twittering of birds feasting on berries in the hedgerow. It seemed to her that she had never felt happier by herself than she did now. Perhaps she had attained contentment and peace of mind at last.

Suddenly a bicycle rounded the bend at breakneck speed. There was a horrible squeal of brakes and the front wheel missed her by inches, but the shock unbalanced her and she ended up in a patch of nettles. Sara yelped and got to her feet immediately to avoid being stung, but there were already a few hits on her legs and arms. Rubbing them ruefully she looked up at the cyclist, who had dismounted, and found that it was Liam O'Connor. His green eyes were full of concern as he held out a hand to help her out of the nettles.

'Oh Lord, I'm terribly sorry! There's not usually anyone in the lane at this time of the morning, and . . . will you listen to me, trying to make excuses?

I'm a clumsy oaf, and I was going far too fast, and I humbly apologise.'

Sara gave him a sorrowful grin, her hand still tingling from the touch of his, and nodded at the rusty bike. 'Do you have a licence to drive that thing?'

His eyes twinkled back at her. 'D'you think I'd get one? To tell you the truth, it's my dad's old bike and I'm not very used to it, but I was in a hurry to get to Seamus O'Clare's place. More haste, less speed, as they say. Here, let me find you some dock.'

'Dock?' Sara stared at him, mesmerised by the sheer vitality of the man. He was bending down to pull up great spotted leaves which he began rolling in his palm.

'Yes, nature's remedy for nettle stings, didn't you know? Now show me where it prickles.'

Resisting the urge to be rude, Sara pointed to the patch on her right leg that was already turning red and itchy. He squatted down and squeezed out some juice from the squashed dock leaves which he applied to the sting.

'There, that should do it. What about the other leg?'

When Liam had anointed all her affected parts he got to his feet and rescued his bike, which he'd thrown down on the opposite verge. He stood holding the handlebars but made no move to go, asking instead, 'Where were you off to this fine morning, Miss Sara Kingston?'

'Just down to the shop ... Hey? how do you know my name?'

'Oh, I know a deal more about you. I know you're here for a painting holiday, but some folk

170

suspect you're nursing a broken heart. I know you've taken one of the McGuires' cottages for a month with the option to extend it, and that you like early morning walks when the dew's still on the grass. I know that Irish music brings tears to your eyes and that you dance with a nimble grace even though you don't know the steps. And I know that you're falling in love –' For a heart-stopping moment Sara thought he even knew about her dream. But then he went on, grinning cheekily, '– with this beautiful country of ours, Mother Ireland.'

She laughed. 'You've got a cheek, Liam O'Connor.'

'So you know my name too? That's a good start. But can't you postpone your shopping trip for a few hours and come with me? I think you'd find it very interesting. I'm off to meet Seamus's cousin, Mick. He's over here on holiday from the United States and he knows a great many Irish songs and dance tunes, so I've been told. Would you care to come along?'

It was an invitation she could hardly resist. Smiling happily, she walked with him, holding on to one handlebar while he held onto the other. It felt safer with the old bicycle between them. Sara listened to Liam's deep, lilting voice as they went along, seduced into silence by his manly presence, by the dark hair that danced freely in the wind and those fascinating green eyes.

'So you see, in America they have kept some of the old music intact,' he was saying, when she finally made an effort to listen to his words instead of being distracted by his voice. 'They know different versions from the songs we know, and I

171

suspect some of them are more original. Not all, mind, because there has always been traffic to and fro, but that's what is so fascinating to work out.'

'You're a music student?' Sara asked.

He laughed. 'I'm studying Irish lore – culture, if you like. That means music and words and legends and customs. It's all so mixed up, you see. There's often no point trying to separate it. Here you have a story or a poem, there you have a song about the same thing. And the tune for singing mixes with the music for dancing, and the rhythm of the words is the same rhythm for the feet, and ... oh Sara, it's all such a wonderful maze to wander in, with so many delightful surprises round every corner.'

Liam's dark brows were raised in quizzical challenge. She felt her cheeks burn, her heart stutter out a warning cry that it was already too late to heed. This man had her in the palm of his hand, and he knew it. He was conquering her with his Irish charm, his Celtic wit, leading her into that wonderful maze where, once lost, she would never want to escape.

The morning spent in Seamus O'Clare's little cottage was remarkable. Out came the whisky, even though it was before noon, and the three men sat round talking all at once, or so it seemed to Sara. Every so often one of them would get up and perform a few dance steps to make a point, or sing a few bars in their rich tenor voices. Once or twice Mick took out his pipe and played a theme which Seamus picked up on his fiddle. They talked of things Sara had no knowledge of, but it didn't matter.

They went to the pub at lunchtime and soon the

older men were chatting to others in a crowd, leaving Liam and Sara alone in the corner. He began to ask questions and she told him that her marriage was breaking up and she'd needed to get away, to think about how she wanted to spend the rest of her life. She opened up, prepared to talk about anything except her lottery win. For some reason she felt embarrassed to mention it, even ashamed. It was so nice to be just an ordinary person again.

'So you gave up your career in art when you got married?' he prompted.

'Yes, I suppose so. I needed a steady job to help pay the mortgage and I didn't want to go through teacher training. I always thought I'd continue to paint as a hobby, but somehow it faded away.'

'What did your parents think about it, after seeing you through college? Were they disappointed?'

'I . . . I don't have parents.'

She saw his eyes cloud. He asked, gently, 'You mean, they've died?'

Sara shrugged. 'I've no idea whether they're alive or dead. I was born illegitimate and my mother gave me away at birth. I often wonder about her, what she's like.'

'Have you made any attempt to find out?'

Sara shook her head. Usually it was painful even thinking about her mother and what she must have gone through, but somehow she knew that Liam understood. No man could sing with such feeling, such poignancy, without being a sensitive soul. She felt drawn to him, and yet wary too, sensing that he wasn't the type for a casual fling. Any woman who became involved with Liam

173

O'Connor would be taking on a complex man with deep feelings.

Sara did her shopping and ended up with two heavy bags that Liam volunteered to carry for her. As they walked back to the cottage, he told her that he would be busy writing up his notes for the rest of the day, but he offered to show her some of the countryside if it was fine, the next day.

'I have the use of my dad's car. I'd love to show you some of my favourite places, Sara. There are some magical spots around here. You could bring your paints and I'll take my fishing rod. We'll be perfect silent partners.'

'That sounds marvellous.' She smiled.

Liam deposited the bags on the scrubbed pine table, declining her offer of coffee, then left in a bit of a hurry. Sara wondered if he felt awkward being alone with her in the cottage. There was a definite chemical attraction, which she was sure he felt too, and yet he seemed to want more of her company. Already she felt she knew him better than to imagine that he might be playing with her affections, but what did he want from her? He was a mystery, as full of past secrets as the green hills, and she longed to get to the heart of him. But would he let her?

In a restless mood, Sara tried to paint the scene from her window that afternoon but her heart wasn't in it. There was no television in the cottage so she dipped into the small collection of books; then, after a light supper, she had a bath and an early night. Once again she dreamed of the Celtic warrior with the emerald eyes, but this time he took her to a round hill where there was a narrow tunnel dug straight into the hillside. She had to crawl on her hands and knees, but inside was a room lined with stones that was big enough for her to stand upright. The warrior laid her down in a stone tomb lined with moss, and solemnly placed a heavy rock over her as a lid.

Sara felt paralysed with panic. In her sleep she tried to move but she felt trussed and bound, stifled inside the narrow confines of the sarcophagus. The air was stale and she could hardly breathe. But just as she was sure that she was going to die the lid was suddenly lifted off and bright sunlight streamed in through a shaft. There beside her was the handsome warrior, completely naked but with a crown of leaves on his dark brow. His penis was erect and proud, making her long to feel its hard length inside her.

Smiling now, the warrior helped her out and onto a softer bed of rose petals that had been prepared for her nearby. She drank the sweet wine he gave her and, as she sank down beside him, he enfolded her in his strong arms and they began to kiss. She knew that this was her reward for choosing life over death, and soon she felt his long member slide into her unresisting vagina like a sword into a well-oiled sheath. In perfect rhythm, they moved slowly towards a mutual climax, her whole body vibrating with prolonged pleasure until she could no longer tell where her flesh ended and his began.

Sara awoke to find sunlight flooding into her room. She sat up in a daze and remembered what a powerful dream she'd had. It seemed more significant than usual, her body still hot and trembling with arousal. For half an hour she lay there recalling the details, so she would remember it always. Had she been initiated into some ancient earth mystery? The melancholy beauty of the landscape had been working its spell on her ever since she arrived, feeding her soul with material for dreams, and now it had borne fruit.

Liam arrived promptly at ten, as arranged. He tooted on the horn of the ancient Morris traveller and Sara emerged in her chain-store jeans and pink anorak, clothes she'd bought in a hurry before leaving England. Although the sun was bright there was an autumnal chill in the air, so she looked askance at the wicker picnic basket in the back.

'You surely don't expect us to eat alfresco on a day like this, do you?'

He gave her a challenging grin. 'Of course! We Irish are a hardy breed. But if it rains we can eat in the car, as a concession to your English wimpishness.'

Sara aimed a reproving tap at his cheek but he caught her wrist midair and held it there while his eyes bored into her, their expression disconcertingly unreadable. Once again she was reminded of his strong virility, of a masculinity all the more powerful for being rooted in feeling. At once she was reminded of her Celtic warrior and she felt her cheeks grow hot as she recalled the unbridled sensuality of the dream. For a few seconds, fantasy and reality merged as she felt his fingers burn into her flesh, right over her faltering pulse, a clear indicator of her latent desire for him. A flicker of recognition passed between them, increasing her embarrassment, and when he finally let her go she placed her hands demurely in her lap and stared straight ahead through the fly-spattered wind-

176

screen as he put the car into gear.

For a while they drove along in silence, climbing steadily. Sara was lost in the abundance of the roadside vegetation, the hedges full of rosehips and blackberries, while the lush green of the hills beyond drew her eye up to the open sky. She was conscious all the time of Liam's animal presence, felt the heat emanating from his body and smelt the fresh-air smell of him. Sitting there in the front seat, she felt enveloped by his aura, overwhelmed by his resemblance to the man of her dreams.

Suddenly he said, without looking at her, 'What is your dream, Sara?'

She stared at him, startled out of her reverie. Wh – what do you mean?'

'Everyone has to have a dream, don't they? Like the song says, if you don't have one, how can it come true? I just wondered what yours could be.'

Sara wanted to say that she longed to find her perfect lover, the one who would forge such a deep bond with her that she would never have to doubt him. Instead she said, 'My dream is to find my mother.'

'Ah.' He was silent for a few seconds, thinking. Then he said, 'It can be done these days, so I believe. Have you taken any first steps in that direction?'

'Not yet.'

'Well, it will be an important quest for you, Sara, and I wish you well.'

'How about you? Do you have a dream?'

'Oh yes. I dream of setting up a school.'

'A *school*? You want to teach?'

He grinned, his teeth white and even between the wide, brownish-pink lips. 'It would be a school

177

of Irish lore, a kind of folk academy. There would be a library of the old tunes and folk tales.'

'That sounds wonderful.'

'But, unlike your dream, it would cost a great deal and I can't ever see myself raising that amount of money. All I can do is keep on collecting and comparing in the hope that some day someone may make use of my labours.'

'Are there no such records already?'

'There's a huge national archive, to be sure, but I'm finding links between the singing, the dancing, the playing, the literature and the old folk ways that are new and exciting.'

'Will you write a book about it?'

'I have to write my thesis first. For my doctorate.'

'Oh yes, of course.'

She'd forgotten that he was a formal scholar, a student of Dublin University. He'd spoken as if this were his life's work, not just a means of acquiring a PhD. His enthusiasm was infectious, especially when she remembered the plaintive sincerity of his singing and the burning light in his eye as he'd danced.

They turned off the lane into what was little more than a footpath and Liam parked the car by a five-barred gate, saying, 'Shall we walk?' Then he helped her to climb over into the field.

The day had clouded over and Sara did up the zip of her anorak as they began to stroll towards the high hill on the horizon. At first it felt odd to be walking beside a man without holding his hand, but after a while she liked the feeling of being separate, yet together. All around, the fields were dotted with ancient oaks and the lush pasture was being grazed by angelic-looking cattle. By the time they reached the lower slopes of the hill, however, clouds had completely covered the sun.

'It's a shame the sun's gone in,' she commented. 'Do you think it will rain?'

He squinted up at the sky. Dark clouds were massing in the distance and Sara thought she heard a low rumble. 'I don't think it's going to be picnic weather, if that's what you mean. But I guess my dad's fruitcake will taste good wherever we eat it.'

'Your *dad*'s fruit cake?'

'Oh, he's a wonderful cook is my dad – a particularly dab hand at cakes. Always puts in a generous measure of the Guinness and a tot or two of whisky. His Christmas cake will knock your socks off.'

Big spots of rain had begun to fall, making great fat splotches on Liam's jacket. The downpour intensified almost at once, making Sara squeal in protest as she struggled to tie on her hood. Suddenly a firm hand grabbed hers. 'Come on; let's make a run for it!'

She followed blindly, wanting only to get out of the storm that was soon raging overhead. Ragged flashes of lightning were followed in seconds by ear-splitting thunderclaps and Sara began to feel afraid. It was a long time since she'd been out in such a violent storm and, with so many trees around, she was scared that one might fall on her. On and on she ran, clinging to Liam's hand while her feet slipped on the wet grass. Then, halfway up the hill, he stopped.

'Quick, in here,' he said.

Sara looked up through the stream of water in

front of her eyes and saw that Liam was half-disappearing into a stone-lined passageway leading right into the hill. She hesitated, but he beckoned her to follow him. Bending her head to avoid the low lintel, she went forward with hunched shoulders into darkness.

'It's all right, I have a torch,' he told her, lighting it at once so that she could see the way ahead. 'There's a chamber at the end of the tunnel. You'll be able to stand upright, soon.'

'What is this place?'

'Some say an ancient burial mound.'

'Oh, my God.' She had remembered her dream. Had it been some kind of premonition? The chill that swept down her spine had little to do with the sudden change in temperature.

'Don't worry, you're safe with me. I'll make sure the leprechauns don't get you.'

Sara was in a dream again, the same as the one she'd had in the night – except she knew that this was reality. Her heart was ranting in her ears, warning her not to go forward into the unknown, but she was powerless to turn back into that terrifying storm. She was truly caught between a rock and a hard place.

'Nearly there.'

Liam's voice was reassuring in the semi-darkness, but his very presence reminded her of a different kind of danger. She trusted him not to harm her, but could she trust herself not to do something stupid? She must take care not to be seduced by her fantasy and identify him with the man of her dreams, or she would only embarrass them both.

It was a relief to reach the inner chamber. The

ceiling was unexpectedly high and the rough-hewn walls comfortingly solid. There, in the heart of the hill, the storm could rage outside till kingdom come and none of its fury could be heard or felt. But Sara gasped aloud when she saw what was in the centre of the worn dirt floor. It was a kind of stone sarcophagus, similar to the rocky bed she had lain on in her dream.

'No, it's not a coffin,' Liam said, registering her shock. 'At least, I don't believe so. There's never been any evidence of remains or grave-goods. I'm in agreement with those scholars who believe it was set up as a place of initiation.'

'Initiation?'

The chill had returned to her bones. Should she tell him? She wanted to, with all her soul, but she was afraid of mentioning her dream in case he grew too curious. How could she tell Liam about her Celtic warrior without betraying her feelings about him? It was impossible. Yet she felt the sweat coming out on her brow and her whole body started trembling uncontrollably.

'What is it?' Liam came towards her and her body shook all the more. Her teeth were chattering too. He put his arms around her and still she shivered. 'You're not claustrophobic, are you?' he asked solicitously. She shook her head. 'Are you wet through? Poor dear. Perhaps we should have run back to the car, not into this place, but I thought it would be nearer. And I meant to bring you here anyway.'

'No, it's not that.'

Sara clung to him desperately, feeling the weird atmosphere of the place seep into her mind and attack her senses with confusion. Flashes of her dream kept returning to torment her. And beneath it all was a hard core of desire for Liam, a desire so strong that it made her dizzy and faint, like a starving beggar within sight of a feast to which she has no invitation.

Looking up, Sara found his face dark and unrecognisable, his eyes such a deep emerald green. Her whole being seemed to yield before his gaze, and she reached up in desperation to touch the wet stringy locks that slithered like snakes through her fingers. He was exuding a seductive essence of manhood that both filled the cave and invaded her heart like a mist. She drew his head down towards hers and his neck bent with a heavy sense of inevitablity, his eyes closing into two dark crescents as his mouth came down onto hers.

To feel his tongue moving inside her mouth, aiming for her throat with the full thrust of male energy behind it, was the purest bliss. With Liam's strong, warm arms surrounding her, Sara felt as if she had entered a cave within a cave and her body sank into his, her soft breasts squashing against his hard chest. A wave of sensual energy was building up in her, making her tingle with longing from head to toe, her nipples and clitoris hard and buzzing.

Had she ever desired a man so much? Sara could not believe that she had ever wanted Guy like this, with every nerve and cell of her body crying out for that sweet union with his. On and on went Liam's kiss until she thought she would faint from erotic rapture, her knees giving way beneath her and her body held upright only by the sheer strength of his embrace. Liam was plundering her mouth with his tongue, drinking in her saliva and making her lips thrill with the subtle changes of pressure as his mood changed from passionate to tender and back again.

Sara felt the tension building in her and knew that if he continued the kiss much longer she would be unable to control herself. If he tried to lay her down, like her dream-lover, and take her right there on the cold, hard ground, she would be powerless to prevent it. It was what she wanted: to have the ultimate knowledge of him, the dark, mystical secret of his manhood. The very thought of it made her womb shudder and her vulva swell, intensifying her arousal to fever pitch.

His lips were light and titillating now, brushing deliciously against hers and making her sigh with frustrated longing. Sara pressed her mons hard against his thigh and felt her clitoris bringing her close to the edge of endurance, her orgasm just seconds away. She wriggled some more and the first warm, satisfying tremors filled her with the certainty that she was about to come. It was incredible, but as the first spasms swelled to a crescendo Sara knew that he had succeeded in bringing her to a climax just by kissing her. That had never happened to her before. She collapsed against him, sure he must be able to feel her wild pulsating and see the flush that bathed her face and neck.

But if Liam did notice, he said nothing. His lips drew back slowly and when she opened her eyes Sara saw the look of confusion on his face. Rocking unsteadily, and with her pulse still hammering, she clung to his forearms for support when he tried to step back.

'God, Sara, I'm so sorry,' she heard him say. 'I didn't mean that to happen.'

Sorry? She almost laughed aloud. Didn't he realise what a great gift he'd just given her? Apparently not, because he was muttering the old 'don't know what came over me' line and she came down to earth with a thud, almost literally. The minute he succeeded in stepping away from her she had to take a grip on herself, to avoid falling onto the rocky floor. Her legs were still weak, but she managed to remain upright, and only then could she take in what he was saying.

'You must think I brought you in here on purpose to seduce you, but that's not so, I swear it. Please say you believe me.'

He seemed genuinely distressed. Sara forced a smile. 'I believe you. Maybe this place is bewitched or something, and put a spell on us.'

She sensed his mood lightening. He grinned at her. 'Maybe it's just that I've been without a girl-friend for a while and you were extremely tempting. But I'm not going to take any more risks of that nature, I promise you. Shall we go out and see if it's still raining?'

As they turned to leave, Sara asked, 'What's this place called?'

'*Tuambru Tuathal*, which means, "the palatial tumulus of the Tuatha". They were a mythical race; the raven warriors, early invaders of Ireland. But the place was probably named long after it was constructed.'

'*Tuambru Tuathal*!' she repeated, loving the rhythmic lilt of the Gaelic brogue.

The outer world seemed centuries away from that ancient time capsule. Leaving it, Sara felt a profound sadness. They came out to find the land-scape washed by the rain and now steaming beneath the sun, looking incredibly green and fresh.

'Too wet for a picnic,' Liam announced. 'It'll have to be the car after all, I'm afraid.'

Sara watched him as she walked a little behind his striding figure, returning to where they'd parked the car. He seemed diminished by the daylight, no longer the mythic figure of her dreams but just an ordinary Irishman. Sara felt incredibly disappointed. She wanted to tell him what had happened to her there in that primeval barrow, to share with him the impassioned drama of her dream, but she knew that the words would sound banal now that the moment of heightened experience had passed.

It didn't stop her wanting him, though. As they sat in the little car, eating and drinking, with a rainbow shining in the misty sky before them, Sara found it incredibly difficult to stop herself from throwing her arms around him. He was talking about life in Dublin, recommending that she should visit the city and discover it for herself, and all the time she was thinking. If you asked me, I would go with you; I'd follow you to the ends of the earth, if you wanted me to.

After they'd finished the soda bread and goat's cheese, the fruitcake and apples, washing it all down with whisky-laced tea from a flask, Liam said that he had to get back.

'I've more notes to write up and photos to file,' he told her. 'It's a job and a half, keeping track of everything. Maybe you'd like to come and see my collection of old photographs sometime?' He paused, his face darkening, then he laughed. 'Oh dear, that does rather sound like a come-on, doesn't it?'

Sara put on a brave face. 'I'm not afraid to look at anything you care to show me, Liam. I'm a big girl now.'

'Mm, I can see that.'

His gaze roved naughtily over her pert breasts, but she pretended not to notice. Flirting with him was just too arousing, and being so close to him was bittersweet, giving her ideas as well as palpitations. He'd made it plain that the incident inside *Tuambru Tuathal* would not be repeated and she was too proud to let him know that she would welcome a repeat performance. So she sat in miserable silence, wondering if it wouldn't be better to break off all contact with Liam O'Connor, rather than yearn continually for what she could not have.

Chapter Eleven

LIAM'S FAREWELL WAS short and sweet, confirming Sara's suspicion that he was as embarrassed as she was about what had occurred inside the tumulus. After vague promises to meet again, she hurried up the path of the little cottage and went in without looking back. Once she was inside, however, she leant against the door and did nothing to stem the tears that began coursing down her cheeks.

Her dream warrior. She'd found him – only to discover that he was too dedicated to his work to get involved with her. Liam's manner had made it clear that his studies came first and he wasn't going to let any woman, let alone an Englishwoman, stand in his way. There had been a moment's aberration that afternoon, but sanity had soon been restored and it would never happen again. That was the clear message Sara had got, without a word being spoken, and now the only course for her was to stay out of harm's way.

But it would be hard to go back to her hermit-like existence, to forget that Liam O'Connor had ever held her in his arms, pressed his lips to hers and started a chain reaction that had led to the erotic equivalent of a nuclear explosion. Sara went to take a bath, then sat drying her hair by the fire and looking through her portfolio of sketches and paintings. If work proved enough of a distraction for Liam, then it might do the same for her. She cast a critical eye over her efforts and came to the conclusion that Ireland had inspired her.

She couldn't remember ever doing such good work before, not even when she was a student. There was a new boldness about her drawing and a self-confidence in her use of colour. Sara knew that it had come from not giving a damn, from not trying to prove anything. She was painting because she loved to, because she found the countryside so beautiful that she wanted to make her own unique record of it, that was all.

And now she wanted to make a painting of *Tuambru Tuathal*. It was clear in her mind's eye; she needed no photographs. She took out her materials and, with a sweep of her wrist across the paper, soon had the familiar outline of the hill in place, together with the mysterious, dark opening to its hollow womb. She added some oak trees to the fields, painted on a wash of green and also coloured in a leaden sky, rent with a great jagged flash of brightness. She would paint the storm as a symbol of her passion and the lightning would stand for her powerful, electric climax.

For hours Sara worked on the painting, adding touches of detail as she recalled them, staying up late into the night with no thought for the needs of her body. When she dropped her brush in exhaustion, she realised that she had a raging thirst and hurried to take a beer out of the fridge. She glugged it down and then made herself a sand-

188

wich. It was almost one o'clock and she'd been working nonstop since four in the afternoon. Drugged by the desperate need to record her vision, she had entered the timeless world of the artist, which resembled the ancient domain of myth and history, the two converging in the subject of her painting.

She slept deeply that night, and if she had dreams she was mercifully spared their recollection. In the morning she woke refreshed and decided to take the bus along the coast, to paint some seascapes. After being out till three in the blustery weather she returned to find a note on her doormat. It was from Liam, inviting her to call at his father's cottage if she wanted to see his photographs.

Sara's heart wanted her to go, but her head warned against it. Probably Liam was just being polite, she told herself, since he had no idea of the depth of her feeling for him. She decided to ignore the note and put a pizza in the oven. While it cooked, she prepared herself a salad and was sitting eating her meal when there was a knock at the door. Thinking that it was one of the McGuires, she got up and answered it.

Liam stood on the doorstep holding a large, leather-bound album, his grin not quite as confident as usual. Sara stood open-mouthed, as if she'd seen a ghost.

'Good evening, Sara, may I come in? I don't know if you were intending to come round this evening, but my dad has his drinking cronies there so it's no place for a young lady tonight. Besides, I reckoned if the mountain will not come to Mohammed, then Mohammed must come to the

189

mountain. I hope you have no other plans. There are some photos in here that I particularly wanted you to see.'

'Well, I'm not sure . . .'

'Oh, you're having your tea? I'm sorry. I didn't mean to intrude.'

Sara recovered her wits. 'It's all right, I've nearly finished. Would you like a cup of tea or coffee?'

She was conscious of sounding like a vicar's wife, even thought she felt more like a lovesick teenager. As she put on the kettle, Liam made himself at home, sitting comfortably in the rocking chair that stood by the fire and placing the heavy volume on his knee. Seeing him so perfectly relaxed in the cottage made Sara wonder if he'd been there before. Perhaps he made a habit of seducing its occupants, she thought uncharitably.

'Milk and sugar?'

'Just one sugar, please.'

The charade continued, with Sara longing to tell him exactly what she thought of him but unable to do more than utter pleasantries. Her whole body was keyed up in his presence, reacting on an animal level that she could not hope to control. Just the sight of his relaxed bulk with his long legs stretched out, rocking the chair back and forth, was enough to make her want to scream with frustration.

'So, how are you enjoying yourself here in the cottage?' he went on conversationally. 'Have you done much painting?'

'Quite a bit.'

She glanced towards the one she had been working on, laid out to dry on top of a cupboard. He followed her eyes and was up in an instant, taking it down. Holding it at arm's length, he squinted at it thoughtfully.

'By God, Sara, you've captured the place wonderfully. Don't tell me this was all from memory?'

'Yes, actually.'

'Then you've a marvellous eye, that's for sure. But there's more to it than faithful reproduction. You've put a good deal of the magic of the place into it, but I'll be damned if I can see how you've done it. That must be the mark of a real artist. I congratulate you.'

Sara shrugged, unwilling to reveal what she really felt about the scene. Impatiently she decided to get the object of his visit over with, so he could leave. 'What are these photos you wanted to show me?'

Slowly he opened the heavy book. 'See? Victorian photographs of the tumulus.' She squatted down beside the chair and peered at the faded, sepia prints. 'It was only discovered in the 1890s. The entrance was completely overgrown, so people thought it was just a hill. But there have been legends about fairies inhabiting the hill for centuries, with tales about people being spirited away.'

'What's this?' Sara asked in surprise. There was a picture of a Victorian gent sporting a handlebar moustache and holding aloft a large sword.

'Ah, that's the Sword of Tuambru. It was discovered in the tumulus by that man, Bernard Monaghan.'

'But I thought you said there were no grave-goods found?'

'That's a matter for debate, but I personally

believe it was not buried with any Celtic chieftain. I think it was always a ceremonial weapon. It was found in a niche in the wall, covered over with a carefully shaped rock.' Liam hesitated, then brought something out from his pocket. 'And so was this.'

He held it out on his flat palm. The object was some kind of buckle in the shape of a horse's head, fashioned as seen from the front with bulging eyes and flared nostrils. It seemed to be made of solid silver. Sara stared at it in amazement and the hairs on her neck prickled. The image of that wild-eyed horse was so close to the charging steed she had seen in her dream, the one the Celtic warrior was riding when he pulled her up to ride with him.

'Mr Monaghan missed it when he found the sceptre. There was another small hole beyond it, also hidden by a stone that fitted into the rock like a piece of a jigsaw. It was only when I went in there with a divining rod that I found it.'

'*You* found this?' Sara reached out and took it into her own hand. It was heavy and cold, beautifully fashioned. 'How old is it?' she asked, breathlessly.

'Oh . . . About three years.'

'What? You're joking!' She looked up and saw him laughing at her.

'No, it's perfectly true. That one's a replica, you see. When I found the original, I handed it in to the curator of the Celtic Antiquities section in Cork museum. They were so impressed by my honesty that they had it copied for me to keep. Apparently, I could have got thousands for it on the international black market.'

'So the original's in the museum?'

'Yes, on display with the sceptre, where it should be. Mind you, I'm not sure they've got the description right. The curator and I are always arguing about it. He takes the Monaghan line, but I believe it was used to fasten a ceremonial cloak. One day I hope to find some moth-eaten old manuscript to prove him wrong.'

Sara gave him back the buckle, still mesmerised. Once again she was being affected by Liam's powerful presence, her nervous system going into overdrive at the sight, smell and sound of him. It was sweet torture to be so near to him and yet unable to throw herself into his arms. She began to wish she'd made some excuse – washing her hair, for instance – and not let him in.

'You seem very interested in the tumulus,' Liam went on, his green eyes searching hers with an intensity that made her very uncomfortable. 'Why is that?'

'I . . . I don't know. It seemed like another world when we were in there. Something more real, more solid, than this one. I can't explain exactly.'

But he seemed to understand. His hand reached for hers, warm and reassuring. 'You are a sensitive person, Sara. An artist, perhaps with a sixth sense or the gift of sight. I knew that, the first time I set eyes on you.'

'You did?' Her mouth was dry and her pulse galloping like a wild horse. He still held her hand in his large, smooth one. She felt dizzy, remembering what had happened when he kissed her. They seemed magnetised to each other, unable to prise themselves apart.

'I sang for you, and only you, at the ceilidh. I wanted to salve your poor, wounded soul.'

'Wounded?' She withdrew her hand, startled. 'What do you mean?'

He looked sad. 'Ah, Sara, you don't have to say anything for a man to see that you've been through some recent trauma. It's written all over your face.'

Sara fought against the urge to tell him everything, about her win and how it had accelerated the subsequent breakdown of her marriage. There was an erotic tension between them so strong that she could scarcely speak. He reached out and stroked her cheek, softly.

'Perhaps I shouldn't have come here tonight,' he said. 'You're vulnerable, and I'm smitten. Not a healthy situation for a man who has a bit of a reputation as a womaniser, wouldn't you agree?'

Sara cleared her throat. 'Is that reputation deserved?' she asked, boldly.

Liam grinned. 'Round here, every red-blooded male who kisses an unmarried girl is regarded as some kind of a Don Juan. We're still living in Victorian times – some might say medieval.'

She regarded him archly. 'So that's all you've ever done, kissed a girl?'

He laughed, a robust sound that filled her soul with optimism. 'Round here, yes. But while I'm away in Dublin – well, that's a different story.'

'You've got a girlfriend there, yes? A fellow student?'

He shook his head. 'Used to have, but she graduated and took a job in Bristol, leaving me in the lurch. Not that I'm nursing a broken heart or anything. Our relationship had run its course, in any case. But listen to me going on. Do you want to tell me about you?'

'Not really. I came here to forget all that.'

'A thousand apologies. I never meant to stir up muddy waters. I'll leave you now, if that's what you want.'

Sara was in turmoil. She said, far too quickly, 'No, please don't go.'

'Are you sure?'

'Yes.' She blurted out, 'You're the best thing that's happened to me since . . . Well, since coming to Ireland.'

He smiled quizzically. 'Well that's a back-handed compliment if ever I heard one, since you've been living here like a recluse ever since you arrived.'

She felt confused. Liam was sharp, and she didn't always know how to take him. But beneath the words there was this undeniable bond, this feeling that they were kindred spirits. 'You're right, I came here to paint, not look for company. And still less for romance. When I saw you at the ceilidh you . . . It knocked me for six.'

'Why?'

'Because of a dream I had.' There, she'd confessed. And she was surprised to feel relief.

'What kind of dream? Was it connected to the tumulus?'

'Yes,' she said, astonished. 'How on earth did you know that?'

'Partly because of what I felt when I was in there with you. A kind of inevitable, overwhelming passion. And partly because of that painting, which only confirmed my feelings.'

There was a significant pause in their conversation, during which Sara felt a deep joy slowly dawning within her. Liam understood! His words confirmed what she already suspected, that her dream had been a foreshadowing of her meeting with him.

He stood up and drew her to her feet, regarding her solemnly. Once again, Sara felt herself enter that timeless space where nothing mattered but the elemental communion of twin souls. When he took her in his arms and placed a soft kiss on her lips, she offered no resistance, but felt all the pain and doubt drain out of her like so much waste energy.

His mouth felt comfortingly familiar now, an old friend, and she let her tongue mingle sweetly with his while his fingers invaded her hair, cutting a swath through the thick locks until he reached her tingling scalp, where his fingertips massaged her gently. His caress was extremely erotic, like the practised touch of a sensual hairdresser who recognises that the scalp, too, can be an erogenous zone.

Sara felt her veins filling with liquid joy as she struggled to stay upright, reeling with the heady sensations that were assailing her from head to toe. Liam sensed her need to be horizontal and guided her over to the sofa bed which he opened up, with a flick of the catch, into a small double. They lay down on it together, using the cushions as pillows, and resumed their slow, exploratory kissing. It was wonderful to feel that, for once, she was setting the pace; that he would take her no further than she wished to go.

'You're so beautiful, Sara, and so sensitive,' he murmured. 'I feel like I've been given an exquisitely wrapped gift. I've already had a little peep inside the parcel, but somehow it's more fun to guess what it contains than to find out for sure.'

'Oh, you've a touch of the blarney about you and no mistake, Liam O'Connor.'

196

'Stop trying to out-Irish me, darling. You're English, you're different. And that's what I like about you. Just be yourself.'

He called me 'darling', she thought gleefully. The word echoed gratifyingly in her ears while his lips sought hers again, more hungrily this time, though still respectful. His hands became more active, stroking her bare arms so softly that the little hairs generated static and crackled against his sleeve. Sara was very aware of her bodily responses, her nipples cresting into firm peaks on her swelling breasts and her pussy melting oh, so deliciously.

The craving within was becoming unbearable and soon Sara just had to feel his naked skin, to know the bliss of intimate contact with male flesh. She began to unbutton his shirt, just the top three buttons, until she could slip her forefinger in and feel the pulse at the base of his throat, just beneath his Adam's apple. His neck was rough, needing a shave, and she rejoiced in the evidence of his virility – not that evidence was needed. Where their crotches rubbed she was teasingly aware of his solid erection, lively as an eel against her belly.

She felt the ancient call of his cock to her womb and a fierce fluttering ensued deep within, almost as intense as an orgasm but not quite. Liam's hands crept to her breasts that were straining for his touch beneath her loose T-shirt. He cupped his palm around one taut curve, caressing the fully erect nipple slowly with his thumb through the thin cotton and making her pussy gush in tremulous anticipation.

Sara explored deeper beneath his open shirt and felt the plateau of his pectoral, fretted with fine hair. Mirroring his actions, she stroked his chest with her palm and let her fingers play over the small, hard nipple, making him groan aloud, 'Oh Sara, sweet Sara, you don't know what you're doing to me.'

'I think I have some idea.' She grinned, opening more buttons until his front was exposed completely. His body was lean and firm, the rippled muscles of his abdomen leading to a slim waist. Acting on impulse, Sara bent her lips to his left nipple and licked at it experimentally. In response, he put both hands beneath her T-shirt and seized both bra-cups, squeezing her breasts gently while his fingertips explored the deep divide between them. She gasped, her libido going into overdrive at this new, tantalising stimulation.

Her lips moved across to his other nipple and, at the same time, a new urge was born. Moving blindly down the shallow valley in the front of his body, licking the fresh salt of his sweat as she went, Sara made her way to his navel, where her tongue paused, while her fingers struggled to undo his belt.

'Here, let me do that,' she heard him say, his voice deep and guttural. It was the tone of a man in too deep to stop. He whipped the leather through the buckle at speed and unbuttoned his jeans with an impatient groan, leaving her to do the rest. Sara eased the zip down very carefully over the long bulge in his white Calvin Kleins and felt, rather than heard, his sigh of relief as she levered his jeans down his thighs so that he could step out of them.

For a few seconds Sara savoured the moment, kneeling before him unashamedly as she put out a tentative hand and felt the heavy sac of his scrotum within its cotton pouch. She looked up to see him standing, erect and proud, his eyes closed in ecstasy as she seized the elastic waistband between her thumbs and fingers, pulling it towards her until his glans popped out and instantly puffed itself up even more with sheer joy at being freed.

It was large and shiny, dark pink in colour and covered with a pearlised film. She felt her mouth water at the sight of it and could hardly wait to take it between her lips. Yet curiosity to see the rest of his cock overcame her appetite and she pulled the stylish pants halfway down his thighs. The shaft of his penis was long, thick and slightly curved and, as Sara grasped the base of it firmly between her thumb and forefinger, her womb contracted with a keen pang.

Moaning softly, she bent her head and licked along the eye of his glans. The first taste of his essence was bittersweet, and once she had anointed him with her own saliva, using the tip of her tongue, she went on to lick and suck him more thoroughly, feeling his juices seep out all the more. Fearing that she might trigger his climax too soon, Sara moved her lips over the whole of his glans and slowly moved her mouth down his shaft until the tip of his cock was comfortably lodged in her throat. Then her tongue moved with agile grace all around his penis as if she were savouring some rare delicacy.

Liam placed his hands on her head like a benediction, completely at the mercy of her mouth. While she fellated him, her hands found the curves of his buttocks and began to knead and stroke them in appreciation of their shapeliness. Like the rest of him, his bottom was smooth and well-toned, testimony to a life of healthy exercise.

Sara felt herself growing uncontrollably hot, her clitoris throbbing wildly as she brought Liam nearer to the brink of orgasm and felt the urgent thrusts of his penis, which she was only just able to contain. One finger slipped down into the crack between his buttocks, following a trail down to his perineum and then on to fondle his balls. She knew she was teasing him, but she couldn't help herself. Like a child in a toy shop, she longed to touch everything, try everything, press this button and tweak that knob. She wanted to possess all of him at once and be possessed by him in turn, but she wanted the ultimate thrill to be mutual, a simultaneous exchanging of gifts.

'If you carry on like that, I'll come.' His voice came from above, strained and distant.

She giggled, wrapping her tongue around his shaft with renewed delight. So come, she thought, see if I care! Her actions became more purposeful; she pumped him with her mouth while she teased his anal opening with her fingertip, feeling the puckered entrance first twitch and then loosen slightly in response to the stimulus. She was sucking him vigorously now, her lips gliding up and down his engorged penis with rhythmic pressure while she tasted the increasingly salty flavour of his glans.

'Oh, dear God, I can't hold out much longer,' she heard him cry, his hips making little thrusting movements into her face. She pulled his bottom cheeks apart and quickly slipped her finger in while he was open and relaxed. His sphincter closed tightly over her index finger, but then his anus softened, allowing her further access. She knew that massaging him inside would make him climax

200

more quickly but she didn't care, it was what she wanted, the full excitement of his ejaculation down her throat. Normally, she would have shied from the experience, but she wanted to do it for him.

Liam gripped handfuls of her hair to steady himself as the final ascent towards orgasm had him rocking on his heels, uttering one long, continuous moan. Sara shuddered within as her lips felt the pulsing along his shaft and the hot, acrid juices spurted into her mouth. She swallowed the lot, ignoring the taste and simply rejoicing in the high-pressured abundance of the flow, which seemed to imply that he hadn't come for some time. His anus contracted around her finger so tightly that it was almost painful, and his thighs were trembling around her cheeks as she gently licked the shaft clean, while slowly withdrawing her mouth.

They collapsed in each other's arms on the floor. Sara's mouth ached and the lingering taste of his sperm was unpleasant, now that the heat of the moment was subsiding, but she was still replete with overwhelming happiness. Liam held her close, his strong hands stroking her hair and her cheek, silently letting her know how much he appreciated what she had just done for him. The idea that he might do the same for her was so exciting that she barely had the energy to think of it. All she wanted was to lie in that sweet cocoon of mindless contentment, basking in the warmth of her lover's body.

In that dozy state, it took Sara quite a few seconds to register the sound of the door knocker. When she did, she sat up in shocked alarm whispering, 'Oh, no. There's someone at the door.'

Liam was already pulling on his pants. 'Answer it, then.'

'I can't. Not with you like that.'

But he was drawing up his jeans at top speed and then thrusting his arms through his shirt-sleeves. Sara looked doubtful, but he waved her towards the door as the banging came again. 'Go on, woman. It might be one of the McGuires.'

Reluctantly, she went to the door and opened it. She gasped in shock when she saw who was standing in the porch: her husband! Staring in blind incomprehension at him, she let his words wash over her like a series of tidal waves, bringing certain disaster in their wake.

'My God, Sara, what on earth possessed you to dig yourself into a hole like this? I've been driving all around the houses, from Bally-this to Bally-that. They said you were here up at the farm, but I had to walk through a bog to get here. Just look at the state of my trousers!'

Guy spoke as if she were somehow responsible, which riled her just enough for her to gather her scattered wits. 'What the hell are you doing here anyway?' she snapped. 'And how on earth did you find me?'

He gave her a sneaky grin. 'You used your gold card from our joint account, remember? You went mad in some department store, down the road. It was easy to trace you once I had the statement.'

Sara cursed her stupidity. She should have realised that she could be traced through her card. A sense of doom threatened to paralyse her. She might have known that her new-found happiness was too good to last. But then her dormant fighting spirit kicked back and her stance grew resolute, barring the door. The memory of how she felt about Liam brought her comfort and strength. She would do all she could to prevent a confrontation between the two men.

'Well, you've wasted your time coming all this way,' she told him, coolly. 'Because I've no wish to talk to you.'

The stubborn look she hated came into his eye. 'Oh, come on, Sara, I'm still your husband. I have a right to see you. There are things we need to discuss.'

'Then let's do it through our lawyers. Goodbye, Guy.'

Sara backed over the threshold, preparing to slam the door in his face, but he was too quick for her. Angrily, he thrust her aside and forced an entrance, almost pushing her to the floor. She recovered in time to see Liam standing in the middle of the room, with his shirt open to the waist and looking as dishevelled as if he'd just got out of bed. There was a confused mixture of emotions registering in his body language: his brows were raised in quizzical inquiry above narrowed eyes, while his mouth was fixed and resolute. His fists were clenched at his sides and his feet set firmly on the floor, standing their ground.

It was amazing how quickly Liam had recovered from the state of sensual languor he'd been in just seconds before. Guy, stopped in his tracks, made an odd snarling sound like some beast confronted with an enemy that might, if luck was on his side, become his supper. Liam's eyes flashed dangerously and his jaw tightened. With an agonising pang of tenderness, Sara realised that he was preparing to do battle for her, if necessary.

Chapter Twelve

THERE WAS DEFINITELY something primitive about the way the two men were squaring up to one another, and Sara felt an equally primitive excitement energising her whole body, turning her on. Somehow the aggressive stance taken up by her husband and lover made the confrontation seem like a Hollywood shoot-out: good guy versus bad guy. Guy's face was contorted into mean rage, while Liam's expression was merely one of puzzled concern, giving him an endearing little-boy look.

At first Sara felt like laughing at their clichéd postures, but then Guy snarled, 'What the hell are you doing here with my wife?' and she knew that he meant business.

She went up and placed a restraining hand on his arm. 'Guy, listen. You've no right to barge in like this.'

He turned his attention to her, his face softening. 'Look Sara, this is madness. I want you to come back to England with me, right now. I made a mistake, a big mistake, and I want you back. Mother wants you back, too, and so do Mark and Penny. They all said we should try harder to make a go of our marriage.'

'So you've had a family conference about me, have you?'

'Not really. But I know they're right – we were meant for each other. And now we've won the lottery we can do anything we want. Only we must do it together, darling.'

'Lottery?' Liam stepped forward, his frown deepening. 'You never told me you'd won the lottery, Sara.'

She was furious with Guy for spilling the beans. 'I didn't want you to know, Liam. I didn't want anyone to know, not here. I came to Ireland to be alone, to think things through and decide what to do with my life. I never expected to meet you, and I never expected Guy to follow me here.' Anger and misery welled up in her, in equal proportion as she blurted out, 'It's all so bloody stupid! I don't need any of this. All I wanted was to be alone.'

Suddenly she wanted to be far away from both men. She grabbed her jacket and ran from the house before either of them realised what she was doing. Seconds later, she was driving her car along the lane, not caring where she went so long as it was as far as possible from the cottage. After a while, realising that she was going at a reckless speed, she slowed down and ambled along the twisting road until she took a left turn and found herself heading out towards *Tuambru Tuathal*, the way Liam had taken her just the day before.

It seemed a lifetime ago. Dusk was falling and the great shadow of the hill was in front of her, vaguely menacing. Yet it was calling to her, too, as if it held some secret clue to the resolution of her problem. Sara drove up to the field gate where they had parked the previous day and got out of the car. The wind was chilly, and she buttoned up her jacket, wishing that she had brought her thick coat instead. Her legs were bare beneath the jeans, and the sandals she wore indoors were on her equally bare feet.

This is madnes, she told herself, climbing over the gate regardless and starting on the track that led directly up to the hillside. Her toes were soon frozen but she carried on doggedly, her eyes on the shrubby thorn bush that hid the entrance from casual passers-by. As she walked Sara knew that she had to go in there again, into that dark womb, even though she had no torch on her and no food or drink.

What if the tunnel collapsed while she was in there and she was walled up alive, only to suffer a lingering death? Sara shuddered as she began to climb the hill but her footsteps did not falter. She reminded herself that the place had withstood the test of time and there was no reason why it should cave in just because she was inside, but it was scary all the same. She reached the entrance and paused to get her breath. The low tunnel stretched like a black hole leading to a bottomless pit, daunting and forbidding.

Ignorant of whatever force was urging her on, Sara began to make her way in, feeling the rough walls of the tunnel and walking warily in case she stubbed her unprotected toes. The place smelt damp and musty and the tunnel seemed far longer than when she had explored it under Liam's protection. At last she was aware of being in the chamber and, after a while, her eyes became used to the darkness and could make out vague shapes. She saw the stone coffin-like box in the middle of the floor and thought: What if Liam was wrong and there was a warrior buried here? What if his ghost still haunts the place?

It would be easy to terrify herself with her imagination, but Sara resolutely refused to do so. She sat on the ground with her knees huddled up to her chest and closed her eyes. A blissful peace came over her, a sense of having escaped from all the pressures of her life. Let those two men fight it out, she thought with a faint smile; what did she care? They were both so different, but perhaps neither was suited to her.

Yet the more she tried to banish thoughts of Liam, the more he seemed to take possession of her mind. What must he think of her? No doubt Guy was telling him all sorts of lies right now. One thing was certain: her sojourn in Ireland must come to an end. She would pay the McGuires handsomely and then quit. Where would she go? Nowhere seemed safe. Although she had enough money to travel anywhere in the world, Guy could catch up with her through her gold card. She really must do something about that.

Such thoughts buzzed around ceaselessly in Sara's brain until she felt dozy and rested her head on her knees. The place was so quiet and still, a haven of tranquillity in a noisy world, that it had a soporific effect on her and in a matter of seconds she was deeply sleeping, worn out by the tensions and exertions of the past few hours.

Sara was awoken by a sound that made her start awake, then stand up in alarm. It was the unmistakable noise of feet kicking against loose stones and it came from the tunnel. Now she could hear a slow, rhythmic tread and it was coming nearer. She squashed herself against the wall in fright, adrenaline rushing through her body and all her pulses hammering. Was it Liam? Or Guy? Or someone else; some stranger who would have her entirely at his mercy? She tried to calculate how long it would take her to make a run for it back down the tunnel once the invader was in the chamber. But how fast could she run, bent almost double?

The light preceded him, whoever he was. First there was a faint yellow shadow, and then a more robust bright circle, on the ground. Into the cavern it came and flashed around in a large arc, coming to rest on her face. Sara squinted and put up her arm to shield herself, both from the light and from possible attack. She was so scared that she was almost wetting herself.

Then came the soft Irish accent she'd come to know so well. 'Sara! I knew you'd be here.'

'Liam! Thank God it's you!'

Sara launched herself into his arms, drawing comfort from his low chuckle and the warm circle of his embrace. She was shivering, her teeth chattering uncontrollably, and he wrapped something dark and thick and woollen around her. Never had she felt so warm and safely protected, not even in childhood when she'd always been just one among many. Now she felt special, precious.

When Sara stopped shivering Liam drew her over to the stone trough where he whisked the woollen material from her shoulders, claiming it back. In the dim light of the torch, which was propped up against the wall and throwing eerie shadows, she could see that he was wearing the horse-head clasp as it should be worn, to fasten his cloak of Irish plaid. She gasped as the light caught the silver horse-face at his breast, recognising her dream warrior. A fatalistic feeling took hold of her, making her shiver at the thought that, just as she'd felt that she was getting herself together, events were spinning out of her control again.

She watched helplessly as he unfastened the clasp and drew off the cloak with a flourish, laying it down in the sarcophagus. Before she realised what was happening he had scooped her up into his arms and was laying her on the soft folds of his cloak. Sara squealed in alarm as he began to strip her methodically of her clothes. He pulled off her jacket, then drew her T-shirt over her head. Without wasting time on the fastenings of her bra, he simply ripped it off her, the flimsy lace tearing in front so that the two cups hung uselessly, exposing her pale, heaving breasts.

'What are you doing?' she murmured, terrified. 'Surely you wouldn't rape me? Not here? Not now?'

For a moment he paused, and the stillness was absolute as he stared down at her with gleaming green eyes. There was nothing to fear in his face, and Sara felt foolish that she had doubted him. Her heart grew warm and tender, filled with more longing than she'd ever felt for any man before.

Liam smiled, saying softly, 'Whatever I do to you, Sara, it could never be rape.'

She knew then that he was right. If he made love to her she would welcome it, draw him into her with a lover's delight. Even the thought of it made her womb dance for joy. Hastily she undid her jeans and pulled them off by herself, leaving the last protection of her modesty for him to remove.

Before he did, Liam began to strip himself in a

languid, casual fashion that had her biting her lip in suspense. She watched his shirt fall to the floor, revealing the strong chest that she had touched and kissed only a few hours before. Then he slid the leather of his belt through his buckle and pulled down the zip of his jeans. He stepped out of them neatly, throwing them into the corner, and she saw the tented bulge in the front of his pants. Knowing what treasure lay inside, Sara felt her vagina gush in tremulous anticipation as he put his hands under the elasticated waistband and slowly exposed himself to her, his erection full-blown and looking magnificent even in the wan torch light.

'Oh God, Liam,' she exclaimed in a small, choked voice.

Tentatively, Sara reached out beyond the stone confines and touched the warm, living flesh. It jerked a little in her hand, testifying to Liam's desire for her. She knew that this time it must be all or nothing, and for a few seconds she hesitated. Maybe this would be the one and only time they would make love, an intense but transient experience that she would remember for the rest of her life. Maybe she was running other risks.

But somehow she trusted this dark warrior of hers more than she'd ever trusted anyone before, even Guy. It felt so right, even here in this dank and gloomy setting, as if some long-forgotten drama were being re-enacted, sanctifying the place. Full of a sense of wonder she took hold of his slim hips and pulled him towards her, tacitly giving her consent. Never before had consenting to anything seemed so momentous.

Quickly Sara slipped off her cotton panties so that she was totally naked, and Liam did likewise.

Then the pair embraced inside the cold tomblike walls. It was a fairly tight squeeze with not much room for foreplay, but they were both beyond such niceties. What she knew he wanted, as much as she did, was for him to come straight into her and join their hungry bodies with a single, thrusting stroke. She opened her knees and he manoeuvred himself between them, his cockhead at the moist entrance. They sighed in unison as he plunged first the glans and then the shaft through the wet fleshy lips and into the plush softness of her interior.

She embraced him wholeheartedly with the muscled walls of her pussy, stroking the long, thick wand with rhythmic pulses that soon had him groaning in ecstasy. For a while he lay still, letting her do all the work, and she reached down to feel the velvety scrotum with its heavy contents, massaging his balls gently through the loose skin. The root of his shaft was hard up against her clitoris, and the upward thrust inside was pressing just as hard on her G-spot.

Much as Sara wanted to savour the moment, to feel him filling her completely while she rippled up and down the rigid length of his cock, the urge to move became too strong and she began to wiggle her mons around, revelling in the increased throbbing of her clitoris. She was soaking wet, too, so much so that she was afraid he might slip out if she moved too violently. Confining herself to subtle thrusts of her pelvis and contractions of her inner muscles, Sara felt Liam's lips crush down on hers, almost knocking the breath out of her, in a kiss of extreme passion. His hands found the hard nubs on her breasts and tweaked them mercilessly, taking her even further along the path towards orgasm.

Soon she could contain herself no longer and her womb began fluttering in spasm, sending ripples of pure pleasure through her body, one after the other, making her cry out in a long paean of joy that echoed around the roof and walls of the ancient cavern. She could feel Liam kissing her face and neck with abandon, kissing even the lids of her closed eyes with his soft lips, murmuring that he loved her, that he had at last found the woman of his dreams.

Yet he stayed firm and still inside her while the erotic storm raged around his penis, stalwart in its erection. Sara had the impression of dancing around it, her quim all flowing and water-like while his rod remained, rooted in her, biding its time. Once her own climax had faded into a tingling glow Liam began to move, slowly at first and only an inch or so at a time, sliding easily back and forth in the sweet fluids that the gushing tidal wave of her orgasm had left behind.

For a while she lay passively quiescent, relishing the slow sweep of his cock as it caressed her inwardly, then she stretched out her legs to ease their cramped ache. With her thighs closed she felt him moving more keenly against her clitoris and the excitement returned, urging her to want more and more of the thrilling friction. Liam seemed to sense her need and sped up the action, darting in and out of her with practised ease, anointing her clitoris with the juice of his glans as it snuggled within her labia, then slipping back inside her.

The titillating effect of his actions soon had her hovering on the brink of coming again. Sara felt his head bend to her breast and sighed as his mouth caught the erect nipple and sucked there strongly,

212

triggering her off. She arched back into his arms as the wild flurries began, racking through her body with the force of an erotic tornado, setting her soul on fire.

And still Liam remained in total control, his murmured endearments the one sign that he was moved by her display of sensual bliss. Sara's desire for him only increased. Making him come with her mouth had been wonderful, but now she wanted to give him the same total fulfilment he'd given her, to feel his shuddering pleasure find its echo deep within her womb, drawing them as close as two human beings could be.

When she had recovered from her cataclysmic orgasm, Sara began to caress his erection with her moisture-laden vagina walls, moving her hips voluptuously to reinforce the stimulus. Liam gave a sharp intake of breath, signalling that her sensual assault on him had struck home. Emboldened, she clutched at his taut buttocks while she kissed the smooth skin of his neck, pressing his pelvis down towards hers as she pushed upward. His breathing became laboured as he strove to maintain the upper hand, but she knew that his was a losing battle. He might be the very incarnation of a Celtic warrior, but Mars always gave way to Venus in the end.

Running a fingertip along the divide between his buttocks, Sara sensed his crack was relaxed and open and slipped in deeper, reaching the sensitive skin around his anus. She teased him mercilessly there while her pelvis and pussy laboured to plea-sure him in a complex rhythm of thrusts, gyrations and squeezes. Never before had she felt so quin-tessentially feminine, so much the *femme fatale*.

Liam's breathing was laboured, his hips working rapidly towards their goal and making his penis thrust home with powerful strokes. Sara felt her own responses heighten. With his rough chest rubbing against her breasts, the nipples were achingly aroused, and within the niche just below her mound she could feel her clitoris reacting fervidly to the repeated friction. She gave an involuntary moan, feeling herself leaving the comfortable sensuality in which she had been wallowing and advancing towards yet another climax.

This time, her ascent was accompanied by his. Together they sought the ultimate gratification and were soon experiencing it, both separately and in unison, their bodies twin poles between which the ecstatic energy flowed in ever-increasing waves. Sara felt indissolubly bound to him, sharing his nature in a way she never had with her husband. It both thrilled and frightened her as she came out of the rapture, sinking back into the mundane, aware that their bodies were mere flesh and the box which confined them both was of cold, hard stone.

'Sara,' she heard him say, kissing her with infinite tenderness on the brow. She snuggled in his arms but they were not in the most comfortable of beds and soon she felt stiff and sore, moving restlessly as her body cooled.

'Come, it's time to get out of this,' Liam said, clambering over the side himself, then giving her a helping hand. He wrapped the cloak around her while he pulled on his clothes, and she relished its soft warmth. Yet she was becoming progressively sadder as she thought about the consequences of what they had done. Uncertain of the outcome she could only stand there silently, racked by doubt.

He must have sensed her concern because he drew her to him and murmured, 'No regrets, Sara?'

She shook her head, but her heart was still wavering. Quickly she put on her clothes and then followed him out of what now felt less like a tomb and more like a bridal chamber. It was a great relief to be out in the open air, even though night had fallen and it was cold. Sara stretched her arms and flexed her calf muscles, feeling the tormented sinews ease. Then she took hold of his hand and they ran down the hillside and across the fields to where both their cars were parked.

Pausing to recover her breath, Sara felt disappointed that they would have to part. Liam sensed her feelings and said, 'If you'd rather not drive, you can come with me and pick up your car in the morning.'

She welcomed the suggestion and was soon sitting in the front seat of the Morris. But Liam made no attempt to switch on the engine straight away. Instead he drew a bag out from under the driving seat, pulling a Thermos out of it. 'I thought we could maybe do with this. Coffee with a dash of whiskey. Would you like some?'

He had brought some of his father's fruitcake, too, and she ate and drank with relish, feeling much better as warmth flooded her insides. Then Liam said, 'After you'd gone, Guy said he'd be filing for divorce. He called you a slut and me a gold-digger. He wouldn't believe me when I said I had no idea about your lottery win.'

'The bastard! But that's him all over. He attributes low motives to everyone, because that's the way he acts himself.'

'I'm sorry if I've made things worse for you, Sara.'

She laughed at that. 'Worse? How could you say that after what we just did in there?' She looked towards the hill rising into the night sky, its summit crowned with stars. 'I think Guy was probably put out by the idea that you were with me because you liked me, not just for the money.'

'Liked you?' He held her face in his hands and regarded her solemnly. 'I love you, Sara. Be in no doubt about that. Whatever else happens, I want you to know how I feel about you.'

'Oh, Liam.' She clung to him, tears in her eyes as she contemplated the fulfilment of her dream. 'Does that mean –' She drew back, bewildered. 'What does it mean, my love? What are we going to do? I haven't given a thought to the future.'

'I have,' he said decisively. 'I want you to stay with me, Sara. Only if you want to, of course. I have a flat in Dublin. It's big enough for the two of us, at least for the time being. I want us to get to know each other better.'

'Me too.' She stretched contentedly in her seat. 'And I want to help you, too. I want to use my money to help you set up that college, so people can study Irish folk music. I've been looking for a project, something really worthwhile.'

But he put his finger to her lips, sealing them gently. 'Ssh, Sara. Let's not make too many plans right now. There are things I want to do for you too, like help you find your mother. But first you have to clear the debris from your life and I have to introduce you to my dad. He has a right to meet the woman who'll be sharing his son's life, don't

216

you think? I want you to regard him as your own father, my darling.'

'Do you think it will work, us being together?' she asked him fearfully, voicing her secret doubts. 'I'm so afraid of committing myself again after what happened with Guy. And what with me having all this money . . .'

'They say that love is a lottery, don't they?' Liam said, with a wry smile. 'Will you take a chance on me?'

His eyes glittered at her in the moonlight, green as the dream warrior's, true as steel, and she knew that they had already pledged themselves to each other. Their love had been forged and purified in the heat of that passion which had united lovers for ever, and would endure.

Other X-rated fiction for women, available by mail: